The Ragpicker

Salem Village - Book One

Pegg Thomas

Spinner of Yarns
PUBLISHING LLC

S PINNER OF YARNS PUBLISHING, LLC
Sault Ste. Marie, Michigan

Copyright @2025 by Pegg Thomas
https://peggthomas.com/
Published in the United States of America
ISBN: 979-8-9929079-1-9
Cover Design by Pegg Thomas – *(Elements of this cover were created using AI technology)*
Cover Art Copyright by Spinner of Yarns Publishing, LLC

This is a work of fiction. Names, characters, and incidents in this book are products of the author's imagination or are used in a fictitious situation with the exception of characters listed in the Author's Notes. Any resemblances to actual events, locations, organizations, incidents, or persons – living or dead – are coincidental and beyond the intent of the author with the exception of those listed in the Author's Notes.

In this series are many actual historical figures. The author has used her imagination to flesh the characters out for the purposes of the series. While using the known facts of the characters, they are not intended to be historically accurate in every detail.

Join Pegg's Newsletter

writing updates – sneak peeks – fiber arts updates – personal
content

https://www.subscribepage.com/PeggThomas

Author's Forenotes

Two towns are referred to in this series, Salem Town and Salem Village. The beginnings of the famous witch trials started in Salem Village, a quiet farming community about three miles northwest of Salem Town. As the number of people being accused grew, the bulk of the proceedings were moved to Salem Town, which was a bustling port city even in the late 1600s. Both were primarily settled by Puritans, but there were also Quakers, whom the Puritans despised.

Conflicting opinions abound on just when the use of *thee* and *thou* disappeared from common use in Colonial America. For clarity's sake, I have chosen to have the Puritans in this series use the pronouns *you* and *your*, while the Quakers will retain—as they historically did—*thee* and *thy*. The Quakers rejected *thou*, considering it too fancy for their preferred plain way of speaking.

The term *goodie* was used as the short form of *goodwife* and applied to a married woman. For instance, today we'd call Goodie Corwin "Mrs. Corwin."

While it looks odd to our modern eyes, in this time period, both men and women who were named after their parents—a very common practice—were referred to as Jr., as in Hannah Jr. and Caleb Jr. in this story. I was tempted to change their names for clarity, but they are real historical figures, so I chose to leave them as they were.

Bible verses are taken from the 1599 Geneva Bible, the version they would have had access to in this time and place.

The *Salem Village Saga* is dedicated to my ancestors:

Caleb and Hannah Buffum
Thomas and Sarah Buffington

I wish I had more details about them and their lives, but I hope my imagination filled in enough to create a good story for my readers.

Salem Village
Fictional Characters

Puritans

Verity Manton
Mary Scudder
Becky Simpson
Joseph Tripp
John Biddle
Jane Biddle

Quakers

Hester Fuller
David O'Sullivan
Isobel O'Sullivan
& O'Sullivan children
Elias Barwick
Arthur Stokes
Phoebe Stokes
Stephen Draper

Salem Village
Historical Characters

Puritans

Thomas Buffington
Sarah Buffington
& Buffington children
Rev. Samuel Parris
Elizabeth Parris
Betty Parris
Abigail Williams
Dr. William Griggs
Rachel Griggs
Elizabeth Hubbard
John Indian
Tituba Indian
William Good
Sarah Good
Alexander Osborne
Sarah Osborne
Rebecca Nurse
Mary Sibley

George Corwin
Lydia Corwin
Ezekiel Cheever
Rev. Increase Mather
Rev. Cotton Mather
John Hathorne
Jonathon Corwin

Quakers

Caleb Buffum
Hannah Buffum
& Buffum children

Chapter 1

November, 1691

U NCLE WILLIAM WAS DEAD.

Like Momma and Papa had gotten dead three years before, although Verity Manton could barely remember them. They were shadowy figures who sometimes visited her in her dreams, along with her baby brother and sister. She didn't like those dreams because she awoke crying and sweating and fearing Indians.

But Indians hadn't killed Uncle William. He'd just withered away, even though he'd not been an old man. The doctor called it yellow fever, but to Verity, it had more to do with the vomiting and flux than the yellow tinge to her uncle's skin. A person could live with yellow skin, but not if he couldn't keep anything inside.

She might be only eight years old, but she knew that to be true. No matter how hard she'd tried, what broths she'd made or what teas she'd brewed, he'd lost everything she'd spooned into him.

Verity had done her best, but it hadn't been good enough.

Men shoveled dirt into the long hole holding the plain wooden coffin as rusty leaves swirled around the opening. The sheriff's wife, Goodie Corwin, held Verity's hand. Just the two of them watched, and Verity only knew Goodie Corwin from seeing her in church. There were no other mourners, not that Uncle William hadn't been a good friend and neighbor. People stayed away because they feared the fever.

Dirt thudded on the lid of the coffin until it was covered. Uncle William hadn't been afraid of the dark, unlike Verity. He'd often comforted her when the bad dreams came, never lighting a candle, just holding her and telling her that God loved her.

She'd never hear his voice again. A shudder passed over Verity, but no tears came. She'd cried so many already, maybe they were all gone.

Goodie Corwin's hand tightened around hers. The kind lady stayed beside her until the last shovelful of dirt had been patted into place, sealing Uncle William away forever. Then she knelt to Verity's level.

"There is a woman coming to claim you." Goodie Corwin had a kindly face and gentle eyes, but the line of her mouth said she didn't like what she was saying. "I fear we could not locate a relative, but Widow Scudder has taken in many orphans before, I am told. She will give you a home."

Verity pulled her hand away and crossed her arms. "I do not know her." Oh, why did Uncle William have to die? She didn't want to be alone, but she didn't want to go with a stranger either.

Goodie Corwin touched her shoulder. "She lives in Salem Village. 'Tis a lovely place, mostly farms, and they have their own church now with a proper Puritan preacher installed, a Mr. Samuel Parris." She mustered a smile. "He has a daughter very near your age. Perhaps you will find a friend in her."

A friend? Like Patience before... before the Indians. But Patience and her family were buried near Momma and Papa. "What is her name?"

"I have not had the pleasure of meeting her, but I am sure introductions will be made at services on Sunday."

The girls in Salem Town had not taken to Verity, an outsider from the wilds of Maine who lived with a bachelor uncle. At first, grief and fear had kept her clinging to Uncle William, even during services, although it was most unusual for a girl her age to be so clingy. The adults had been tolerant of her emotional distress.

The children had only seen her as different—in a society where conformity was a virtue.

And when the dresses Momma had made grew too small, Uncle William had bought hand-me-downs from the most gossipy woman in the church, whose five daughters had tormented Verity about it. It'd been easier to stay in the house and work at the tasks she knew, tasks Momma had taught her before the Indians, like sweeping and scrubbing and washing clothes. Uncle William had praised her on what a fine job she'd done on his shirts.

Tears blurred the face of the woman in front of her, so they weren't all dried up yet. "I would like a friend."

"I know." Understanding filled Goodie Corwin's voice. "'Tis why I agreed that Salem Village would be a good change for you." She smoothed Verity's wayward hair back under her bonnet.

"Is this the girl, then?" A scratchy voice interrupted them.

Goodie Corwin straightened, keeping one hand on Verity's shoulder while looking over her head. "Are you Widow Scudder?" Her words were something between a demand and dismay.

Verity turned, dread climbing her throat like a squirrel up a tree.

"'Tis my name." The woman was older than anyone Verity knew. Her hair was covered with a scrap of cloth tied beneath her chin, not a proper bonnet, and her face held more wrinkles than a spring apple. Her dark eyes were almost lost in the folds, and when she spoke, no teeth graced the puckered opening of her mouth. "Is this the girl I am to take away?"

"I was led to understand that you took in orphans." Goodie Corwin's fingers tightened on Verity's shoulders. "I assumed you to be a younger woman who—"

"'Tis the older who need help, not the younger." The old woman sized Verity up with a sharp glance. "She will do. Come, girl." She extended a gnarled hand.

Verity shrank back against Goodie Corwin.

"Ah, Widow Scudder, I see you have come on time." Sheriff George Corwin, one of the men who'd buried Uncle William, approached, carrying the sack of Verity's belongings they'd left near the grave. He cast an uneasy glance at his wife. "Is anything amiss?"

"'Tis only that I had a different idea about who would—"

"And I told her, I have need of the help." The widow thrust out her hand again. "Come, girl. 'Tis a long walk back to Salem Village."

The Sheriff handed Verity's sack to the old woman. "I am sure everything will be fine. Widow Scudder knows what a child needs. She has years of experience with them."

"That I do." The old woman opened the sack and peered inside.

It contained everything Verity owned, and she wanted to snatch it back, but she couldn't move. Her body was numb. Her mind was angry, which she knew to be a sin, and sinning was wrong. So she welcomed the numbness.

"Come, my dear." The sheriff held out his hand to his wife while bowing to Widow Scudder. "If you will excuse us, we must be on our way. Good day to you." He eased his wife away.

Goodie Corwin gave Verity's shoulder one last squeeze, a pressure that echoed in Verity's throat. "All will be well," she said as her husband led her away with hasty steps.

Verity wanted to run after them. Even though she barely knew them, they were her last link to Uncle William. But the numbness wouldn't let her.

Widow Scudder grabbed her arm in a pinching grip. "Come on, girl." She slung Verity's sack onto her back. "You belong to me now. Do as you are told, and we shall get on fine."

The Corwins were already out of sight on the other side of the church.

The cross from the steeple painted a dark shadow on the grounds of the churchyard, pointing to Uncle William's grave. Verity wanted to go back and say goodbye one last time, but Widow Scudder set off in the other direction.

There was no one left for her in Salem Town and nothing for her to do but take one numb step at a time after the old woman, who didn't release her arm.

The sun hung low in the west and slanted shadows across the dirt street of Salem Village. It was nothing like Salem Town. For one thing, Verity couldn't smell the ocean. It smelled more of forest and fields, like her old home in Maine.

Grief welled over her even as she followed Widow Scudder. She pulled her tattered shawl—Momma's old shawl—tighter across her shoulders. She missed Momma and Papa and Uncle William so much, it hurt in the center of her chest. And the tears she'd thought were dried up had dribbled down her cheeks several times during the walk to the village.

Her feet were sore. The numbness had worn off, and her too-tight shoes were pressing against her toes. She needed a larger pair. Uncle William had said he'd buy her a new pair for winter, but then he'd gotten sick. And died.

The widow hadn't said a word to her for the entire journey, but she'd released her grip on Verity's arm early on. Verity had no trouble keeping up with the old woman, whose steps shuffled in the colorful leaves.

The village was a collection of whitewashed buildings, including a church with its steeple pointed heavenward and businesses with painted boards out front swinging from ropes or chains. Verity couldn't read, but most had pictures to show what they were. And the blacksmith shop had open double doors. The heat and light from its forge spilled into the street, its acrid scent lending a sting to the air. They passed house after house, at least two dozen of them, most made of milled boards with porches and steps out front. Some were only log structures that again reminded Verity of Maine.

Widow Scudder didn't slow or even look around. The old woman's mouth drew a puckered line, and Verity was afraid to ask where they were going as the houses receded behind them. It didn't really matter. She had nowhere else to go.

In the distance, at the edge of the forest, long past the last house on the street, squatted a dark shack. Or maybe it was dark because the shadow from the forest covered it, the sun sinking below the treetops. Widow Scudder's steps, slow though they were, never wavered.

Verity's heart sank. It would be dark in that shack. There was only one window on the front, a very small one, and no light glowed from inside. The even darker forest lurked behind it. Did Indians live there?

"Where are they?"

Verity startled at the scratchy voice beside her.

"Jumpy little thing, you are." The wrinkle-rimmed eyes skimmed over Verity again. "But I suppose you got reason enough. I am sorry your uncle died, child."

Words wouldn't squeeze past the tightness of Verity's throat, but she managed a nod.

"You behave, do as you are told, and all will be well." The old woman snorted. "But I suppose you will run off and find mischief for yourself like the rest of them."

Working up all her courage, Verity cleared her throat. "Who?"

Widow Scudder waved a hand at the forest shrouded in darkness. "The other orphans who live with me and work for me, as those who did before."

"There are others?" A small gleam of hope crept into Verity. She wouldn't be alone with the old woman.

"Two at the moment, but the Lord only knows where they have gotten themselves off to."

Verity never wanted to be the reason the widow's voice took on that ominous tone, nor to cause the old woman's mouth to crease into its fearsome scowl.

They reached the shack, which the widow called a cottage, and it was as dark as it'd looked from the distance, lacking any sort of whitewash. Lacking a porch, the building seemed to settle directly onto the forest floor. The widow pushed open the door that hung from leather hinges, and Verity stepped inside onto a packed dirt floor.

With the door shut behind them, the feeble light from the only window cast an eerie shaft across the single room's sparse contents. A wattle-and-daub hearth took up most of one wall but held no welcoming flame or heat. Against the opposite wall, a narrow bed sagged under a tatty brown blanket. The back wall held four wide shelves stacked in pairs, with more blankets wadded on top of them. A square table stood in the middle of the room, with benches along two sides. One chair sat near the hearth. A handful of large baskets hung from the rafters, along with bundles of herbs, ears of dried corn, braids of onions, dried fish, and strings of dried green beans. The building smelled of dirt and fish and old things.

"Light a fire, girl." Widow Scudder pointed to a box half full of wood.

Verity knelt beside the hearth, knees pressed into the soot and dirt, and stirred the gray ashes until she uncovered a dull ember. She leaned over and blew on it until it glowed, then added small bits of bark until it caught. She added slivers of wood until a little blaze was going.

"Someone taught you well enough." The widow's voice still crackled, but there was a faint undertone of approval.

"Momma did."

The old woman sat on the chair with a thump and a heavy sigh. "What is your name, child?"

"Verity Manton."

"Pretty name." The dark eyes gleamed in the fire's light as she examined Verity again. "How old are you?"

"Eight years old this past August."

"Mmm-hmm." The old woman rubbed her chin. "You are a pretty one. That never hurts when asking for scraps."

"Scraps?" Did the widow expect her to beg for food? Uncle William had given to the poor who sometimes came to the house, so she'd seen beggars. Verity wasn't a beggar.

"Aye, child. We all have to work together here if we wish to eat."

Verity was used to working in the house. Momma had needed her help after her brother and then her sister were born, and especially after her brother had died of illness. Momma had suffered from melancholia for many weeks after his death. Papa had been so worried.

Then the Indians came, and Verity only survived because she'd been sent to the fort for a bag of salt to brine pickles. If she'd been home, she'd be in the churchyard in Maine with her family. Instead, she'd gone to live with Uncle William and keep house for him.

If only she'd died with her family, she wouldn't be in a gloomy shack in Massachusetts with a frightful old woman she didn't know.

"You will be our ragpicker, little Verity." The old woman nodded as if satisfied with her announcement.

Verity shook her head. "I cannot be a ragpicker."

"Whyever not?"

"Only the very poor and the infirm are ragpickers."

"Child." The old woman spread her arms as if to show off the shack's single room. "You *are* very poor now. 'Tis time to get used to that idea. We all work or we do not survive. You will beg for scraps of cloth, food if anyone will give it, and scavenge where you can. Becky will unravel the rags for their threads, cook, and keep house. You and she can untwist the threads in the evenings. Joseph will keep the woodbox filled, fish in the stream, tend traps for meat, and make the journey to Salem Town to sell the untwisted fibers to the papermaker there."

Verity's knees trembled as she rose. "From whom will I beg?"

"The townswomen, the local farmers, the merchants—it matters not. There is a dump on the town's eastern edge to scavenge from as well." She shook a gnarled finger at Verity. "But you stay away from the Quakers, girl. Those people are the devil's own, you hear me?"

Verity nodded. After all, she'd always heard it was best to avoid them. Everyone knew they were sinners on their way to hell for their ungodly ways.

The old woman held her hands out to the flames, then rubbed them together. "You must learn quickly. Winter is almost upon us."

The meager supplies hanging from the rafters would not be enough to feed a single person through the cold months, much less four.

The door opened, and a gust of cold air rushed in. A girl entered, older than Verity, but not yet on the edge of womanhood. She had long dark hair pulled back and covered with a cloth much like the widow's. Her eyes were dark as the night, and her skin pale enough to give her an almost spectral appearance. She removed the head covering and glared at Verity.

Behind her came a boy with a thatch of uncovered hair the color of straw. Upon seeing Verity standing by the hearth, his wide grin exposed bright teeth and a dimple on each tanned cheek. The two couldn't have looked more opposite of each other, although both were thin to the point of skinny and wearing clothing long past its prime.

"Becky, Joseph." Widow Scudder pointed at each as she said their names, then to Verity. "This is Verity—our new ragpicker."

The shame of that title settled on her narrow shoulders like a weight of condemnation. What would Uncle William have thought? Or Momma and Papa? She'd tried so hard to be good, but it hadn't been enough. And now she was to be nothing more than a beggar.

Chapter 2

"**S**HE CAME INTO TOWN last evening with another orphan in tow. A little girl who looked frightened half to death." Hannah Buffum set a bowl of venison stew on the long plank table in front of her husband. "I wish we could do more to help."

"Thee know as well as I that Widow Scudder will take nothing from us." Her husband waited while Hannah set five more bowls around the table in front of their children and dished one up for herself. "Let us pray before this fine food grows cold."

In the manner of their Society of Friends—called Quakers by most—they bowed their heads for a silent prayer. The quiet of the house settled around them and peace filled Hannah's heart, as it always did when contemplating the things of heaven. When Caleb cleared his throat to signal the end of the prayer, the homey sounds of horn spoons scraping wooden bowls replaced the silence.

Hannah Jr., their eldest, sat to her right. Old enough to be married at two and twenty, she was yet content to stay on the farm and run the dairy. There might be another reason, but

Hannah refrained from asking, since it would likely create an uproar she didn't want to deal with. So Hannah Jr. remained, creating cheeses that were prized around the colony. Enough so that even many of the Puritans would purchase from her.

But not Widow Scudder. The old woman was dead-set against the Friends. She'd take a handout from anyone else—even sent the orphans to beg for her—but never from one of them.

The vision of that poor girl following the widow through town plagued Hannah. "If only that old woman would accept a wheel of cheese from us, or even a bucket of milk from time to time. Children need milk to grow and be healthy."

Benji and Jonathan, her two youngest at ages five and three, both grabbed their pewter cups of milk and took long swallows. With milk coating their upper lips, they returned to spooning up the stew. They were growing well and were hardy lads, a testimony to her husband's prosperous farm, and a vivid contrast to the frail orphans the old widow kept.

Caleb pushed his empty bowl back and grabbed the last slice of bread from the plate in the middle of the table. "Thee are wise, goodwife." He took a bite and chewed, keeping eye contact with her until he swallowed. "I am not unfeeling toward the orphans. The Puritans give the widow a stipend for her care of them. I know this for a fact. I suspect, however, 'tis not nearly enough."

"The children are so thin." It wouldn't take long before the new girl was, too.

"Aye, but I have never heard a word about her mistreating them. 'Tis a matter of not enough to eat, plain and simple."

"If only she would—"

Caleb raised his hand to stop her. "We have been through this before. I have tried, thee have tried. We cannot force her to accept our charity."

"What if we gave the cheese to another of the Puritans to give to Widow Scudder?" Hannah Jr. asked.

Perhaps that could work. But who would be willing to help them? "Caleb?" Hannah put a wealth of question into his name.

Her husband finished his bread and then planted his elbows on the table in the manner he did when deep in thought. But he turned to their daughter instead of Hannah. "Who would thee have in mind?"

"Thomas Buffington." There wasn't the slightest pause in her answer. She'd obviously been thinking it through while they ate.

Caleb cocked his head at their eldest. "And why would thee choose him?"

Hannah Jr.'s cheeks flushed a rosy hue. She wasn't a simpering lass to not speak her mind, but Caleb's directness had no doubt flustered her. "He agreed to apprentice Robert, did he not?"

Which had left an empty spot in Hannah's heart. Caleb Jr. sat beside his father, but on the other side rested an empty chair. Robert had begun his apprenticeship in September when he'd turned sixteen. Unlike Caleb Jr., who was as brawny and robust as his father, Robert was of a slighter build, quick and nimble with both his fingers and his mind, but he would never have the strength and stamina of his father or older brother to be a prosperous farmer or carpenter. An apprenticeship with a craftsman in the village had seemed the best choice.

But oh, how she missed her boy.

"Indeed, he did. Thomas is a reasonable man." He didn't add, *for a Puritan*, but even twelve-year-old Tamson's brows rose at the inference in her father's voice.

"Then will thee speak with him?" Hannah held her breath, the answer meaning a great deal to her if only to help the pitiful child she'd witnessed the day before.

"I shall. 'Twould be a welcome opportunity to fill the cellar with a few kegs before winter arrives."

"Shall I go with thee, Father?" Caleb Jr. asked.

"And me?" Benji bounced on his chair, always happy for a wagon ride to the village.

"Me too?" Jonathan lisped.

Tamson and Hannah Jr. remained silent, but their eyes sparked with hope of a family outing to town that didn't involve Sunday meeting.

Hannah folded her hands on the table in front of her. "Why do we not all go? I could use some fresh yeast from the brewer."

Caleb chuckled. "Hitch the team, Caleb Jr. But we must return in time for the evening milking. Girls"—he smiled at each in turn—"put on thy best bonnets."

Chair legs scraped the plank flooring and everyone scrambled to make ready.

"Thee are a soft touch, husband." But Hannah went to him and hugged him once the children had left the room. "Thank thee for doing this."

His strong arm came around her, and even after twenty-three years of marriage, her heart warmed in response to his touch.

"I know not which means more to thee, feeding the orphans or seeing Robert."

"Robert is my own flesh and blood. He will always come first."

"But?"

"He is already well cared for, with room and board and learning a trade. The orphan children, they have no one other than Widow Scudder. The old woman means well, I am certain, but the children provide more for her than she does for them."

"'Tis the sad lot of those not blessed with family, I suppose."

"The Bible says we are to care for widows and orphans."

He hugged her tighter against his side and then let her go. "And so we shall. Be ready in ten minutes." He strode out the door.

Hannah hummed as she scraped the almost empty bowls into a wooden trencher and placed it on the floor for Rags, their black-and-white collie dog, to clean up. Even Rags ate better than those poor children.

Please, Lord, let Thomas Buffington see the rightness in assisting us to feed those children—for they are Your children.

The *thunk* of a log hitting the packed dirt floor startled Verity awake. She curled deeper into the single blanket, which held very little warmth on the solid wooden shelf she'd been given to sleep on.

Someone crouched in front of the hearth, stirring last evening's embers to life. A flame licked up and cast the outline of Joseph, lower legs and feet bare beneath his breeches, linen shirt untucked, hair in wild disarray.

Verity relaxed as much as she could while shivering on the cold wood. Her stomach rumbled. She'd eaten nothing before the funeral, and after the long walk from Salem Town, had been given only a small bowl of boiled potatoes with green beans for supper. No bread, no butter, not even a cup of milk. Another shiver raced across her skin.

Widow Scudder snored from the only bed in the room, so Verity eased down off of her top shelf as quietly as she could, keeping the blanket wrapped around her shoulders. She'd slept in her dress, unwilling to strip down to her shift with the others in the shack. It must be a wrinkled mess, but she would have to worry about that later. Warmth was the first thing she needed, and then food.

She passed the other upper shelf where Becky remained beneath her blanket, and joined Joseph at the fire.

"Good morning," he whispered.

"Good morning." She yawned and then stretched her fingers toward the fire. "Is there anything to eat?"

He glanced at the sleeping form of the widow across the room, the fire providing enough light to chase away the darkness. "'Tis best we wait for her to awaken. She calls it stealing if we eat anything other than at mealtimes."

"But I am so hungry."

"I know." He settled another log on the fire. "You get used to it after a while."

You are very poor now. 'Tis time to get used to that idea. The widow's words came back to her, and she shivered again despite the fire. "How long have you lived here with her?"

He scrunched his nose and scratched behind his ear. "I came in the spring, and that was three springs ago. So that would be two and a half years, I reckon."

"What happened to your family?"

"My parents died when I was too young to remember them. After that, my granny raised me, but she was old and just... died." There was no sadness in his voice. It was as if he were talking of someone else. "What about you?"

"Momma and Papa and my little sister were killed by Indians, so I came to Salem Town to live with Uncle William, but he..." She pulled in a half-breath, half-sob. "He died of the fever." She muffled the next sob in her blanket.

Joseph put an arm around her and pulled her against his shoulder. "'Tis going to be all right. You have us now."

Verity leaned into his warmth and comfort. Was this what having an older brother would have been like?

"Better not let her catch you all snuggled up so cozy like." Becky joined them at the fire, blanket wrapped around her.

"Why?" Verity asked.

Becky poked her with a hard finger. "You have a lot to learn. She needs us to work, to bring in food, wood, and whatever we can find to sell. We are not here to be a family, so get that idea out of your head, girl."

"There is no need to be harsh." Joseph removed his arm.

Verity missed the warmth and comfort, scooting farther from Becky. The girl had ignored her the evening before. Maybe she'd keep ignoring her if Verity stayed out of her way.

Becky removed her blanket, then shook it out and put it back on her shelf. Her dress was horribly wrinkled, but she didn't seem to notice. She poured water from a bucket into the pot that hung near the fire, then measured out four handfuls of milled oats from a keg on the workbench under the window. "With another mouth to feed, these will not last long." She swung the pot over the fire, then faced Verity. "You best learn to earn your keep—and soon—or we shall all starve this winter." She pulled a thick shawl off the peg by the door and went outside.

"Worry not about her." Joseph tipped his head toward the door. "She is a sour one. You will do fine as a ragpicker."

"I know not how to do that."

"'Twill be easy for you. The goodwives will be generous when they see your face. Just be sure to smudge it with a bit of dirt, that and your hands. They think a clean child has no need to beg."

"I have never begged before."

"I had not either until I came here." He sat straighter. "And I will not much longer. I will be twelve next spring, old enough to apprentice." He glanced at the old woman in the bed again and whispered, "Old enough to leave here."

"But is not Becky older than you? She is still here."

"'Tis different for a girl."

Becky returned and pulled the door shut.

Widow Scudder snorted and sat, blinking at the three of them for a long moment. "Got the porridge started, girl?"

"That I do, ma'am." Becky went to the hearth and gave the watery oats a quick stir.

The widow rose, also wearing her dress, and came to the fire to sit in the chair near where Verity huddled in her blanket. She smelled of needing a bath, and her clothes of needing a scrubbing. Her hair was long and stringy and hanging down her back.

She fixed her attention on Verity. "Today you shall walk the village with Joseph and learn which places are best to approach. Tomorrow, he will take you around to the farms." She pointed a gnarled finger at Joseph. "You were the silver-tongued one when you were her age. Teach her how to ask for things proper-like."

"Aye, ma'am. I will."

"Girl, fetch me the sack." The widow motioned for Verity to fetch her sack of belongings that she'd hung on a peg near her bed.

Verity hurried to obey, happy to have her belongings in her hands again, but the widow snatched them away when she returned to the fire.

"Let us see what we have of use in here."

"Those are my things." Verity reached for them, but a glare from the old woman had her stepping back.

"We share here, girl. All of us." Her words were a crackly growl that sent fear through Verity. "I share my home, and you share what you bring into it."

Home? The damp, dark, and dirty shack hardly fit Verity's idea of a home for farm animals, much less people. But the old woman was serious.

The widow drew out Verity's spare dresses, the blue and the brown. She wore the gray because it was the closest she had to black for Uncle William's funeral. The old woman inspected every inch of them. "We can sell these for a goodly sum."

"But—" Verity's protest was silenced by the woman's glare, as well as Becky's pinch to her back.

Next came her spare shift and three pairs of stockings. The old woman cackled with glee. "A pair for each of us this winter." She handed a pair to Becky, a pair to Joseph, and tucked the other pair under the sack in her lap.

Was Verity to be left with nothing but the stockings on her feet? Then she noticed again Joseph's bare legs, and Becky's bare feet showing beneath the hem of her too-short dress.

"And what is this?" Verity's heart sank when the widow held up her brass circle shawl pin.

"That was Momma's." She reached for it. "'Tis all I have left from her." She'd been allowed to wear it and Momma's shawl on her errand to fetch the pickling salt, that awful day the Indians came.

The old woman held it aloft, out of Verity's reach. "'Tis the rent you shall pay to live here. The price 'twill fetch in Salem Town will purchase half a winter's worth of ground corn."

Verity's stomach rumbled.

"See there, girl. You are learning. Fripperies are nice, but they fill not your belly." The circle pin disappeared into the old woman's pocket. "Is the porridge done yet?"

"Done enough." Becky pulled mismatched cups from the mantel above the hearth and ladled them full of the thin gruel. She handed them out, and they slurped the meager breakfast without moving to the table or saying a prayer.

Verity looked into the contents of her cup and took a tentative sip. It was tasteless. "Is there no molasses?" she asked.

Becky snorted. "She will fancy bacon and eggs next, I suppose."

Joseph caught her eye and shook his head, so Verity didn't respond other than to drink her portion of the meal. It didn't fill her stomach, but it warmed her and eased the hunger. Maybe that was enough—for now.

Maybe it was the best she could hope for anymore.

Chapter 3

H ANNAH HURRIED DOWN THE street, holding her bonnet against the freshness of the autumn breeze, her yeast pot snugged under her other arm. Russet and gold leaves swirled in the dirt and collected along the porches and steps leading to the businesses and homes of Salem Village. She'd left the children behind with Caleb in the general store, hoping for a moment alone with Robert before they followed her.

Not that she worried he was ill-kept in his indenture, but there were things a young man might tell his mother that he wouldn't say in front of his father or siblings or tell her at meeting on Sunday. And she needed to hear from his own lips that he was happy and thriving in his new position. He'd been gone almost six weeks. Only two miles down the road, to be sure, but for a mother's heart, it may as well have been fifty.

She was almost to the brewer's door when it burst open, Robert holding it against the wind. "Ma!" His tone lifted in surprise and perhaps excitement.

Hannah stepped onto the wide porch that fronted the building, the mingling scents of yeast and woodsmoke and roasting malt surrounding her. They were alone, no one else close enough to overhear. Still, she lowered her voice. "How are thee faring, Robert?"

"Fine. What brings thee here?"

Fine. That was all he had to say? But he looked well, his eyes bright and clear, skin flushed from the warmth of the brewery. Another gust of wind tore at her skirt. "May I step inside?"

The flush on his cheeks deepened. "Of course. Enter, please, and welcome." He stepped back and half-bowed, his arm flung wide to usher her in.

That must be something Thomas had taught him, for it was not an action a Friend would have used. They didn't believe in showing such deference to another person, but the Puritans disagreed with that—as they disagreed with most of the principles of the Friends.

"Thee look well-fed, I must say." She stepped past him into the brewery. Barrels and kegs lined three of the walls except where the windows let in light. The other wall was half hung with tools and half taken up by a long counter.

"Goodie Buffington is a good cook."

"Goodie?" Hannah whirled around to face Robert. "Why do thee—"

He raised a hand to stop her, in a gesture so like Caleb's that she clamped her lips closed. "Mr. Buffington prefers that I use their Puritan titles while under his apprenticeship."

"But at meeting, thee does not." Nor should he. The Friends did not use any honorifics added to a person's name. No person was valued in any way above another.

"Of course not." He grinned at her. "Fear not. I am not about to become a Puritan, only a brewer. I promise."

"See thee holds fast to that promise." She held out her yeast pot. "Have thee any yeast to refresh my pot today?"

"Indeed." He took the heavy piece of crockery. "We have a good working barm on the far vat I can dip from."

She followed him to one of the three large vats, the yeasty smell even stronger deep inside the building. "Benji and

Jonathan are eating their share of bread and more these days. I can barely keep up."

He took a long wooden ladle and scooped some of the frothy liquid off the top, emptying it into her pot. "'Tis because thee bake the best bread."

She took the pot back and replaced its lid. "How much do I owe thee?"

"Not a penny." The booming voice from behind nearly caused her to drop the pot, but Robert steadied it in her hands. She turned and smiled at the brewer.

Thomas looked the part for his occupation, a generous expanse of middle and a ready smile seaming creases in his cheeks. He peered at her from behind round spectacles, his curly dark hair still devoid of gray, although he and Sarah had been married almost as long as she and Caleb. His coat was open, golden waistcoat set off over a pair of dark blue breeches, a gold chain dangling from his watch pocket.

"But I have always paid for the barm."

"'Tis a benefit of your son working for me." He chuckled, a most pleasing sound and rather rare from a Puritan, in Hannah's experience. They tended to be a dour lot, in general.

"I thank thee." She lifted the pot a little. "Both for this and for taking good care of Robert. He seems quite happy here."

A commotion at the door drew their attention before Caleb and the children entered. "A moment only, the lot of thee," Caleb said. "Wish thy brother a good day and then back to the wagon."

Robert rushed to meet them, picking up Jonathan and holding him high while answering a barrage of questions about the things inside the brewery.

Caleb joined her and Thomas. "May we have a word with thee?"

The brewer's brows rose. "Of course. Does this concern Robert?"

"Not at all." Caleb planted his feet and rocked back on his heels. "'Tis about the orphans Widow Scudder has taken in."

"Ah, I see." The brewer looked uncomfortable. "You have no doubt noticed the condition of the children."

"They are half-starved," Hannah said.

"I fear you may be correct." He spread his hands. "The town's benevolence fund gives the widow support, enough to feed the children, but they also require clothing and shoes and other things. The goodwives of the area give as they are able, but you know the condition of this year's crops. The drought is bringing hard times to the village."

"And yesterday," Hannah said, "Widow Scudder brought in another one. I saw her myself, a little girl."

"Our eldest daughter had a notion," Caleb said, "that perhaps the widow would accept the occasional bucket of milk or wheel of cheese if it were to come through thee, for she will have nothing from us."

"Pride goeth before destruction." Thomas quoted the scripture.

"But the children need to eat." Hannah pressed her case. "And even with a poorer-than-normal harvest, we have plenty of milk and cheese. Surely the old woman will take assistance from thee if she knows not that 'twas us who supplied it."

"Indeed. If she has a new girl, I expect she will be to the house soon. The widow gets them out begging for rags while they are young and harder to resist." He chuckled again. "My goodwife can never turn them away without something in their bellies as well as their hands." He leaned closer. "And instructions that the old woman need not know about what went into their bellies."

"Sarah has a kind heart."

"She does, as do you." He turned to Caleb. "Bring what you can spare and leave it here with Robert. I shall see that the children get it. I fear if we sent a full wheel of cheese, the old woman would sell it instead of feed it to them. I know not what she does with her coins, but they do not seem to benefit those orphans."

"Thank thee, Thomas." Hannah hugged the yeast pot close. "Thee have taken a burden from my soul."

He waved a dismissive hand. "'Tis I who should be thanking you for seeing the need and stepping forth to address it."

"We will take up no more of thy time, but if thee have a trio of kegs for our cellar…" Caleb and Thomas strode toward one of the stacks of barrels, discussing the finer points of each brew.

Hannah Jr. joined her and slipped her hand through the crook of Hannah's elbow. "Well done."

"'Twas thy idea, my dear." She patted her daughter's hand. "Thee were wise to suggest it. Pray, do not hesitate to present thy thoughts in the future. Thee have grown into a discerning young woman, one I am most proud of."

"Pride, Mother?" Her lips twitched at the corners.

"In its best form, I assure thee. Come. Let us rescue thy brother and herd the rest out to the wagon." Arms still linked, they left the brewer's shop and stepped back into the blustery fall air.

In the distance, two of the orphans scampered behind the Puritan church. One was the new girl in her gray dress, white shawl, and white bonnet. She could almost pass for one of the Friends in that attire. In age, she would fit between Tamson and Benji. Hannah would take the poor girl in, if given the chance.

But of course, the Puritans who ran the town would never allow one of their orphans to be taken in by a family of Friends.

Verity struggled for breath when Joseph pulled her behind the church building. With her shoulders back against the cold boards, her heart pounded in the grip of fear. "Who are they?"

Joseph peeked around the corner. "Quakers. A whole family of them."

"Did they see us?"

"I know not, but none are coming this way."

"What should we do?"

"Stand still. I will keep watch. If they come toward us, we can run for the creek and hide in the willows and brambles. The leaves are mostly gone, but the tangle of vines will do."

A shudder went through her. "Do they chase you often?"

He looked at her then, brow furrowed. "Nay. They never have."

"But 'tis true they do the devil's bidding, is it not?" That was what Verity had heard before when Quakers were discussed by the adults in her life.

"I guess so." Joseph shrugged. "The Indians left them alone during the uprising, and Widow Scudder says to stay away. If that old woman is afraid of them, I reckon we should be too."

The rattle of wagon wheels had Joseph peeking around the corner again. He relaxed beside her. "They turned around. I think that man is the carpenter who owns the big farm northwest of town."

"Must I...?" Verity clenched the fabric of her dress in both fists. "Must I beg scraps from them?"

"Nay, never there. Widow Scudder never darkens their doors and neither must we. They mostly live on the north side of town, farmers and some craftsmen, so they are easy to avoid."

Verity let out a long sigh. The widow had warned her about the Quakers. She'd never been afraid of people before the Indians had come. She'd never been afraid of anything that she could remember before then. But after that, fear stalked her like a cat after a mouse.

"Come on." Joseph tugged on her shawl. "I will introduce you to the best houses first, the ones most likely to give a *starving orphan* a handout." He stressed the two words that best described Verity at that moment.

Her stomach growled.

"If you can do that when the goodwife opens the door, all the better."

"But I cannot. It just happens when I am hungry."

Joseph stopped. "I know. It was hard for me at first too. You will grow accustomed to it." Then he flashed her a grin. "Some of the goodwives give a small portion of food, enough to eat before returning to the widow's."

"But she said we must all share. What if she and Becky go hungry because I ate something given to me?"

"Verity." He put a hand on each of her shoulders and looked her in the eyes. "You are going to have to learn to look after yourself. The widow says she takes care of us, but God's truth, 'tis we who take care of her."

Verity knew about taking care of others. She'd taken care of Uncle William, but he'd died anyway. What she'd done hadn't been good enough. Even though the widow frightened her, she didn't want the woman to die because of her.

"Come on." Joseph led them around behind the houses to an alley lined with hedges. "Goodie Buffington is a kind-hearted soul. More than once she has given me scraps of cloth with buttons on them."

"Buttons?"

He cocked his head at her. "You will learn. A button is like finding treasure. I can sell buttons in Salem Town for coins. I have a small collection stored in the forest where the widow cannot find them."

Hiding treasure from the widow? That didn't seem like the right thing to do. But neither had it been right for the old woman to take away Verity's dresses. Sharing her stockings with those who had none, that she could understand. But her dresses barely fit her, and wouldn't fit either Becky or the widow. Taking them away to sell them had been wrong. Maybe Joseph was right not to share everything.

He stopped them where the hedges hid them from view from the houses, then reached down and dirtied his hand—which hadn't been clean to start—rubbing a bit on his cheeks. "Go on then. Do the same. You have to look the part."

"What part?" Verity didn't want dirt on her hands and face.

He huffed and wiped his hands across her face, despite her struggles of protest. "There. The part of a poor orphan."

Tears welled in Verity's eyes. She dashed the back of her hand across her cheek, and it came away muddy. "See what you have done?" More tears followed.

"Aw, cry not, Verity. 'Tis just how it is." Then he squinted at her. "Or maybe the tears will bring more sympathy and more handouts. And one thing to remember, always go to the back door. Poor folks never knock on the front door." He pointed through the bushes at a two-story house with a small back porch. "Goodie Buffington's is where we shall start."

But she didn't want to start. She wanted to go home. Home to Salem Town and Uncle William. Home to where she had dresses and stockings and her mother's shawl pin. Home where she'd never been so hungry and cold and... alone.

Chapter 4

THE WHITEWASHED DOOR OPENED, and the scent of roasting chicken engulfed Verity. Despite her tears and fears and unhappiness, her stomach gurgled. Loudly.

"Good day, Goodie Buffington." Joseph sketched a bow, then motioned to Verity. "I brought another with me today. This is Verity Manton, newly come to Salem Village."

"Well, bring her right in, Joseph." The goodwife ushered them into the room with a huge hearth, two chickens trussed and hung near the fire. She squatted to Verity's level. "Welcome to the village, Verity. My, that is a pretty name."

There was nothing but kindness in the woman's voice. Her dark hair was held back under a linen cap, and her brown eyes were as friendly as her voice. They warmed Verity almost as much as the kitchen did. "'Twas my grandmother's name, but I never knew her. She lived in England."

"I see." She turned to a girl at the table in the center of the room. "Abigail, slice a couple of pieces of bread and butter them generously for these two."

The girl smiled at Verity, doing as the older woman bid.

Goodie Buffington focused back on Verity. "I am sorry 'tis not fresh, but 'tis all I have today."

"Thank you." Joseph's voice was wistful, not his usual jaunty self. "We are awfully hungry. But Widow Scudder sent us to fetch any cloth scraps we can find."

"Let me think." She turned back to the girl cutting the bread. "What did we do with the shirt your brother tore last week?"

"'Tis in the mending hamper, but the sleeve is a terrible mess."

"Aye, I remember now. He snagged it in a thornbush in the woods, and 'twas barely worn. We can spare the rest of that sleeve and reuse the remainder of the shirt in a quilt, I think."

"Here is the bread." The girl brought the thick pieces to Verity and Joseph, both lathered with creamy butter. "I will fetch the sleeve for them."

Verity took her slice of the bread. She should wrap it in something and take it to the shack to share, but she had nothing to wrap it in, and Joseph was already devouring his portion. Her stomach cramped, hard this time, and she took a bite. The butter melted on her tongue like warm snowflakes. When had she ever tasted better? She'd just have another bite or two, then wrap the rest in the sleeve to take back.

"Do you have enough firewood for the winter, Joseph?" the goodwife asked.

"Nay, but I am working on it." He stuffed the last bite of bread in his mouth.

Goodie Buffington *tsked* and shook her head. "I could send Thomas Jr. or Benjamin to help on Monday if that would suit you, and if their father can spare one of them a few hours at the brewery."

"That would be kind." Joseph's bread was gone. He wiped his hands down the front of his shirt.

"Here you are, Mother." The girl gave a wad of fabric to the goodwife, who presented it to Verity.

Verity took it, only then realizing that her bread was gone too. She'd eaten every crumb. She swallowed and looked up at Goodie Buffington. "Thank you."

"Come once a week. I will set aside what I can spare for you."

"She will." Joseph was quick to answer when Verity remained silent. "Now I better show her around town."

"Until next time." The goodwife closed the door behind them.

Joseph grabbed Verity by the hand and pulled her along until they were out of sight behind the bushes. "You did great. And a whole sleeve? The widow will be pleased, for sure."

"But I ate all the bread." Verity sniffled back the guilt that poked at her. "I should have saved some for Becky and the widow."

Joseph crossed his arms. "You reckon they are not eating at the shack while we are out here combing the streets for scraps?"

Were they? How would Verity know? The widow seemed as thin as the rest of them. She couldn't be eating much either. Or was she just old-person thin? Verity had seen old people at church who were very thin. It was all so... It was too much to think about. Too much to keep straight.

"Come on. Next door is the midwife, Hester Fuller. She never married or had children of her own, poor woman, but she still has a soft spot for an orphan."

Verity followed, stuffing her pocket with the damaged sleeve. Would she have to do this every day? Trudging through the back gardens of the village, eating scraps from the tables of people she didn't know, and collecting rags?

But at least her stomach was full. For now.

"Come on." Joseph pulled at Verity's sleeve. "I want to show you some houses to avoid unless you must beg there—and only if you have no other rags for the day. One most especially." His voice dropped to a whisper that sent a chill through Verity.

"Are they Quakers there?"

"Nay. William Good is a drunkard, and Sarah Good is a nasty old woman who smells bad and smokes a pipe."

"As old as the widow?" How many old people could one village have?

"Nobody is as old as the widow." His forehead wrinkled. "Not that I know of. Besides, Goodie Good has a young daughter, so she must not be that old. She just acts old because she is mean and cranky."

Goodie Good? With a name like that, one would assume her to be a good woman. Thankfully, Verity had Joseph to keep her from making that mistake.

They walked the length of the alley behind the houses. Most had trees in the back and smaller porches, narrow with steep steps, and many had chickens pecking in the dirt. Joseph didn't stop until they came to the very last one, a two-story house that might have been nice once.

The house looked scary now, its whitewash faded or weathered away, and windows so dirty it was doubtful anyone could see out of them. The porch steps sagged in the middle. The back garden was a tangle of tall grass and weeds withered by the frost. There were no chickens in sight to keep it pecked clean or a fence to contain them. The huge tree behind the house leaned as if a good wind might topple it over, its leafless branches swaying above Verity and Joseph.

She stepped closer to him. "I do not like this place."

"Nor should you." He turned to her, face as serious as she'd ever seen it. "Do not come here unless you have nothing to bring back to the shack. The widow gets angry if you come back empty-handed. 'Tis best to try everywhere else first and approach the Goods' house only if you must."

"Would they give me anything?" If they couldn't afford to keep the house, how could they afford to give away even scraps?

"Sometimes, but 'tis never much and never valuable. You will get no buttons here." He started back the way they'd come. "Follow me. I shall show you the rest of the best houses."

"Will we stop at the reverend's house?"

"Not today. There are others who give more generously. Why do you ask?"

"Someone told me he has a daughter near my age." She didn't want to admit to wanting a friend, because Joseph was being so kind to her. But he was a boy, and it wasn't the same as having a girl for a friend.

"Betty Parris is her name."

Verity skipped forward to keep pace with his longer legs so she could see his face. "Is she nice?"

He shrugged. "I have never spoken to her."

"Why not?"

He stopped then and faced her. "The other village children have no interest in us orphans. Best not to get your hopes up that one will notice you, much less speak to you." He walked on.

After a moment, Verity hiked her skirt and hurried to catch up. Maybe Joseph was wrong. Maybe Betty simply didn't speak with boys. Surely, tomorrow after church, the girls would gather, and she would meet them. That was how it'd been in Salem Town, but of course, she'd been grieving too much to join their circle after church until the damage had been done—and she'd been branded an outcast.

The idea of that darling little girl being forced to beg for rags haunted Hannah during their return to the farm. Getting the children food was the most important thing, but what about the rest? What about making their lives better? Teaching them skills they could use when they were older would benefit them far more than begging. Hannah Jr. could use help in the dairy. For that matter, Hannah could use domestic help in the house with the two little boys.

Caleb stopped the wagon near the front porch and set the brake. "Thee have been deep in thought. Are thee still worried about Robert?"

Their children scrambled out of the wagon and hurried into the house, each carrying a package of their purchases. Only Caleb Jr. lingered. He would assist his father in moving the barrels into the cellar.

"Nay. 'Tis obvious he is in fine spirits and well-fed. He looked quite at home in the brewery. Did thee not think so?"

"Indeed. 'Twould seem an occupation very fitting for our second son. So why thy silence?"

She let out a long sigh. "'Tis the little orphan girl."

"Thee would bring her into our home if thee could. Am I right?"

Hannah gripped his arm. "Might there be a way?"

Caleb shook his head. "I think not. The village elders have the say, and they are not about to give even an orphan Puritan girl into our care for fear we will lead her to destruction."

"As if we believe in a God different from theirs." Hannah pressed her lips together to prevent anything else from escaping while Caleb Jr. listened. He was almost a man grown at the age of ten and eight, but he was still her boy, and she wouldn't speak ill of anyone in his presence.

"I know." A wealth of understanding and comfort flowed through her husband's voice. "They understand us not."

"Nor do they try," Caleb Jr. said.

Her husband turned on the seat to face their son. "Was not our discussion with Thomas productive?"

"I suppose." But there was an undertone of surliness in Caleb Jr.'s response.

"It takes time to build trust between people who believe differently—even people who worship the same God."

As always, her husband was level-headed and sensible, a steady man who could turn his hand to about anything, who could provide well for their family. A man respected in their community of Friends, one often approached for his opinion on weighty matters.

But Hannah wished he'd agree to cross the barriers between Puritan and Friends, snatch that poor child up, and bring her home.

She climbed down from the wagon and looked up at him. "I know thee are right, but I do not have to be content with it."

Caleb released the brake and smiled down at her. "Thee would not be the woman I love if thee were. Have patience. Pray. Ask God to make a way where there seems to be no way." He clicked to the horses and drove around the house to the cellar door.

Pray. An answer that sometimes frustrated her when she wanted to take action, but it was the true answer to every situation. How had she let it slip past her? Pride. Arrogance. Self-reliance over reliance on God. She stopped on the porch, sat on the top step, and bowed her head.

Father God, I am ashamed that I needed Caleb to tell me what I should have done from the start. Thank Thee for waiting patiently for me to ask this of Thee. Please work out—in Thy perfect timing—the opportunity to offer more to the orphans with Widow Scudder. Not only food, but skills they will need. And Lord, please work on the widow's heart to love those children, because food and skills alone are not enough. I pray that the Puritans are teaching them about Thee

*in their church tomorrow, because they—as all of us—need
the Light of Christ most of all.*

Hannah waited a few moments on the step, as was her
custom after a prayer. One should wait and listen for a time
to give the Lord a chance to answer. When no nudge came
to her spirit to do anything more, she rose and entered the
house.

Hannah Jr. had the large willow basket of mending on the
table and was sorting through its contents. She looked up
when Hannah entered. "What do thee think? Can we spare
some of these for the little ragpicker? I could add them to the
basket of cheese for the Buffingtons to hand out."

They saved most of their rags for wrapping the wheels
of cheese while they cured on the shelves in the dairy, so
there weren't many to spare. "What about the old cheese
cloths? Some are quite ratty, but she only needs to unravel
and untwist the threads for the paper maker. It matters not
their condition for his paper."

Her daughter beamed. "I had not thought of that. I have a
stack in the dairy I can fetch." She thrust the mending back
into its basket and grabbed her shawl before scurrying out the
door.

The young woman was very keen on this project. Or was
it the opportunity to visit the brewery again? Hannah Jr. had
been looking around the brewery as if she intended to purchase the lot. A mother noticed such things—like the Buffingtons' twin sons not being in attendance during their visit. Twin
sons three years younger than her daughter, but handsome
lads almost impossible to tell apart.

Had one of them caught her daughter's eye? What would
happen if he had, a Puritan young man and a daughter of the
Friends? Such an attraction would lead to nothing good. Or at
least, nothing easy.

Perhaps Hannah had more to worry about than the little
orphan girl.

Chapter 5

Verity left the outhouse—a frightening structure that leaned to one side so that the door did not close properly—with the anticipation of the church service to come. And the dread.

Her best dress remained in her sack, which the widow kept under her bed. The village girls might accept her friendship if she wore it because she'd look more like them. Widow Scudder had said she'd make the trip to Salem Town in a few days to sell Verity's belongings. But Verity wanted to wear her best dress to church, even if she could only wear it once more. She opened the door of the shack, fumbling for the words to convince the widow to allow her the use of the dress.

"Shut the door. You are letting in the cold." The widow sat by the fire, hunched over in her chair with a shawl wrapped around her. She wore the same clothes she'd worn since Verity had met her, as did Becky and Joseph. Did they not have something special for Sunday services?

Becky slopped their morning porridge into the mugs and without a word handed one to the widow in her chair and set the rest on the table. Verity and the other two sat on the benches. No one spoke as they drank the contents. Verity finished hers, not even tasting it, and then plucked up all her courage. "Widow Scudder, may I wear my good blue dress to church today?"

Becky gaped at her, and Joseph shook his head, and the widow glared.

Verity wrapped both hands around her empty mug to keep them from trembling.

"You have no *good blue dress* anymore, girl. You have no need of it. We here in the cottage do not attend church. Those high-and-mighty citizens of the village have no desire for our kind in their pews."

Trembling or not, and ignoring Joseph's silent pleading, Verity stood. "I am a Puritan like them. I always attend church. 'Tis the right and proper thing to do. Uncle William said 'tis where I can learn of God and learn how to avoid sinning."

The widow's slight figure rocked forward, and a sound emerged that might have been a laugh from someone else. It sounded like two hens in a fight over a choice scrap of food.

Verity didn't move, nor did Becky or Joseph. The very room seemed to hold its breath.

Widow Scudder cackled a few more times, then leaned back and wiped her eyes. "Bless you, girl. If there are any needing to learn of God and how to avoid sinning, 'twould be those who sit in the pews on a Sunday and forget about the orphans and widows." She raised a crooked finger and wagged it. "I know the Bible as well as most. If you have questions, you ask me." She jabbed the finger into her breast, then gazed into the fire and mumbled to herself.

Joseph slid from his bench, grabbed Verity by the arm, and hauled her out of the shack into the early morning light twinkling off the frost-covered ground.

"Where are we going?" Verity had to jog to keep up with his longer legs since he hadn't released her arm.

"Into the forest."

Verity pulled back, digging her heels into the ground. "Nay. 'Tis scary in there."

He let go of her arm and faced her. "'Tis not. There are wonderful places in the forest. Secret places we can go and not be found."

Fear gripped her again, worse than the fear of the widow. "But there are Indians." Even in Salem Town, right on the coast, people had spoken in hushed voices after church of nearby Indian raids.

"I never saw an Indian in there, and I know this forest well."

"It scares me." Verity hugged her shawl tighter and shivered, but not from the frosty air.

"Fear not when you are with me." Joseph straightened to his full height and crossed his arms, one elbow poking through the hole in his sleeve. "I know every inch of this forest, and no Indians live in it. Besides, the widow will not follow us in there."

"Will she not send us out to beg today?"

"Nay. She may be batty in the head about the church, but even she will observe the Lord's day in her own way."

That bit of reassurance made Verity feel better—until Joseph grasped her arm again.

"Come on. I will show you the best hiding places in the forest."

This time, she allowed herself to be led forward. When he dropped her arm, she caught the back of his coat and held on, unwilling to lose contact lest she get lost.

The trees were almost bare of leaves, only the brown ones hanging on, and they rustled in the breeze as if telling secrets above. Towering dark green pines with dense needles blocked the sunlight and added to the gloominess, their bare lower branches sticking out like the bones of a carcass. Fallen leaves and pine needles carpeted the path they followed. Verity tripped over the occasional exposed root. Everything smelled of dampness and decay and the coming of winter.

She wanted to go home. Not to the shack with the widow, but *home*. Only she didn't have a home anymore. If she could have taken back her blue dress and gone to church, maybe one of the goodwives in the village would have taken her in. But no one was going to take in a ragpicker.

A single hot tear traced its way down her cheek, turning cold by the time it reached her chin.

"Why the tears?" Joseph stopped and bent to her level. "What is wrong?"

"Everything." Misery spilled out with that word, and his arms came around her. She leaned against him and sobbed. He patted her back and held her tighter.

When her sobs had reduced to slurpy hiccups, Joseph produced a scrap of handkerchief and wiped her face. He handed it to her. "Blow your nose. You will feel better now with that done."

She blew into the cloth. "I do not."

"You will. I know." He took the handkerchief back and stuffed it in his pocket. "I had to do the same thing when I first came here."

Verity blinked lashes sticky with tears. "You cried?"

He shuffled his feet. "I was a lot younger then. No older than you."

In an odd way, that made Verity feel better. "But you seem happy now."

"Happy?" Joseph rubbed a hand along his chin. "I am not unhappy. And for now, that is enough." He took her hand. "Come on. We shall see my favorite place in the forest."

Verity gripped his hand and followed. Joseph was right. She did feel better. Not happy, but maybe she was also not unhappy. It seemed to be enough for Joseph.

Maybe that was the best she could hope for.

"Listen, ladies." Hannah addressed the women gathered in a social group in the meetinghouse yard. "I have an idea—one I have already begun working on—that will help the plight of the orphan children in Widow Scudder's care."

"Widow Scudder? She will not give us the time of day," said Isobel O'Sullivan, wife of the village gunsmith.

"'Tis how she is." Hannah spread her hands. "But the children are starving and scantily dressed. This past week, she took in another one, a little girl."

Many of the women wagged their heads in sorrow for the child.

"As she will accept nothing from us Friends, what can we do?" asked Hester Fuller, the midwife.

Hannah explained her idea of enlisting the aid of the Puritan women in town, outlining what she'd already worked out with the Buffingtons. "If we each can enlist just one Puritan woman, surely the lives of those children will improve."

"I would take the girl in a moment, would the village elders but allow it." Isobel had eight children of her own, but a heart big enough for more.

"I feel the same," Hannah said, "and Caleb would as well, but we cannot take the child without the consent of the elders. He assures me they will never grant it."

"He is correct." Hester glanced around the circle. "On the rare occasions when a woman has died in a childbirth I attended, and the father is unable to provide for the babe, I have recommended one of our women to raise it." She shook her head. "They will not listen. To them, being given over to a Friend is tantamount to being cast into the devil's fire."

Murmurings broke out in the circle, but Hannah clapped her hands lightly. "Let us not get off track. The elders are who they are, but there are children who need our help. Not every Puritan is as rigid as others when it comes to dealing with us. Surely, we can find those who will help."

"I like Hannah's idea," Hester said. "I shall approach Mary Sibley. She is one who will speak to me. She is not as stand-offish as most, and she has a heart for children." The Puritan ladies often called on Hester when their time came because she had such a good reputation, so many live and healthy babies delivered. Of all of them, Hester had the best chance to break through the religious barrier in the village.

Other women chose more Puritans to approach, and by the time their menfolk had the horses hitched and were ready to leave, the ladies' plan was in place.

Caleb assisted Hannah onto the wagon, then joined her on the seat. The back was filled with their children, including Robert, whom they would drop off at the brewery on their way. Should something befall her and Caleb, Hannah Jr. was old enough to keep the household going, and Caleb Jr. old enough to run the farm. Their children's circumstances would not change much. They would not be penniless orphans left to beg scraps.

Caleb clicked to the horses. "Were thee successful in thy mission?"

"All seem willing to reach out. Now 'tis up to the Puritan women if they are willing to receive."

"Then thee have done what thee can." He glanced at her with an approving smile. "I am proud of thee, wife—not in the sinful way of pride—and happy for the day thee accepted me to be thy husband."

Warmth spread through her at his words and crept into her cheeks.

He leaned closer and whispered, "I do believe I have made thee blush."

Tamson giggled from behind them.

"That is enough in front of the children," she whispered back.

"'Tis all right, Mother," Hannah Jr. said. "It does us good to know that our parents have a high regard for each other."

Was that a wistful note in her voice? Hannah glanced back, but her eldest daughter sat facing the Puritan church with three-year-old Jonathan on her lap.

Caleb caught her eye and raised a brow.

Hannah shook her head. She didn't know anything for certain, but she couldn't deny her uneasy feelings. Perhaps she needed to have a conversation with her daughter—sooner rather than later.

"How much farther?" Verity stumbled over another root and righted herself, her toes aching. They'd been in the forest for hours. "Are we lost?" Her stomach cramped against its emptiness.

"Nay." Joseph pointed ahead. "See that pine tree with the split in the middle as if two trees grew as one?"

Verity peered around him. "I see it."

"Just beyond is my best secret place. Better even than the others."

The others had been nice, but nothing Verity would brave the forest for without Joseph leading her. "What makes it the best?"

"You shall see." He flashed her a wide grin.

They passed the split pine and slid down into a shallow hollow in the forest floor that was surrounded by brambles.

Joseph pointed. "Look there."

A rock wall rose out of the forest floor, its front covered in the prickly brambles.

"'Tis just a rock."

Another grin. "Follow me." Joseph walked up to the rock wall, slipping between the brambles, stepped to the side... and disappeared.

"Joseph?" Verity cried out.

He stepped back into view. "Come on. 'Tis a cave."

Oh, no. Not that. "I cannot."

"You can. Take my hand." He reached for her.

Verity shook her head. "I am afraid of caves. They are dark."

"This one is not. Trust me." He grabbed her hand and tugged.

With all her might, she wanted to pull away and run, but where would she go without Joseph? Could she find her way back to the shack? What if she ran into Indians or a bear? Her stomach in knots between the hunger and fear, she let herself be led to the rock wall, and then stepped sideways through a crack in the rock that opened into a cave.

"See?" Joseph pointed to a circle of light on the dirt floor. "I told you. 'Tis not dark in here."

He had to duck so his head didn't brush the cave's ceiling, but Verity could stand upright. They walked to the light and stopped in its circle on the floor. Above them was a hole, ringed with dried grasses and fallen leaves. It opened into the forest above. The cool breeze shook bare branches overhead but they were sheltered from it.

"Is it not a special, secret place?"

"Aye." She twirled around while looking up. There was a bag hanging from a tree root that dropped from the cave's ceiling. "What is that?"

"The best part for us today." Joseph untied the bag and sat on the cave's floor where a pair of flat rocks rested. He opened the bag and poured out some of the contents.

Nuts. Verity's mouth watered. "Can we eat them?"

"I have been collecting them from all over the forest." He handed her a thick walnut with some of its leathery coating still on it. "Use the rocks to break it open."

It took her three tries, but she cracked it. Joseph handed her a sharp thorn. She pried the nutmeat from its shell and popped it into her mouth. When had anything ever tasted so good? She swallowed, already digging out the other half. With the nutmeat almost to her lips, she paused. "Should we not share these with the widow and Becky?"

Shrugging, Joseph swallowed the bite he'd been chewing. "The widow never told me to gather nuts, so I am not withholding anything she asked of me. The way I got it figured, that means these are mine to share with whomever I wish. And today, I wish it to be you." He cracked another nut, a smaller hickory nut, and handed it to her.

"Thank you." She worked on picking out the nutmeat and chewing it while thinking about his words. They were not stealing from anyone, except maybe the squirrels. Or maybe from God, since He planted the trees. But He'd given them over for people to manage, so it couldn't be a sin to eat the nuts.

They ate in silence, the nuts filling her belly, until sounds reached them through the opening above. Not just a noise. She cocked her head. Voices.

Fear shot through Verity, and she grasped Joseph's coat and stood with him. "Are they Indians?" she whispered.

"*Shh.* Let me listen." He stood until his head was in the opening, but not beyond it. He tilted his head, eyes half-closed. Then he ducked down to her level again. "'Tis not Indians. They are speaking English, but one of them sounds odd."

"Like an Indian?"

"I think not." He tied the bag of nuts back to the protruding root. "Let us go and see."

"Nay. Let us return to the shack." It wasn't much, but it was safer than here with strangers in the woods beyond.

"Come on, they will not see us. Let us find out who they are."

Her choices were to follow him, stay in the cave alone, or try to find her own way to the shack after hours of walking and visiting places in the forest. Whoever was speaking beyond the opening couldn't be more frightening than being alone and lost in the forest.

At least, Verity hoped not.

Chapter 6

V ERITY CROUCHED BESIDE JOSEPH, her knees sinking into the damp forest floor. Visible through a thick hedge of brambles that grew around the trunk of a fallen tree, a tall dark woman spoke to two girls not much older than Verity. She couldn't hear every word, because a breeze fluttered the dry leaves around them, but between gusts, she heard enough to know that the woman was telling a story.

"We should go." Joseph eased away from their hiding place. "Come on."

"Who are those girls?" Verity whispered over her shoulder, not moving.

"'Tis the Puritan preacher's daughter and her cousin."

Verity whipped around and squinted for a better look. "Truly?"

"Aye. Now come before they hear us."

"But we are whispering." Verity didn't budge. Before her was the very person she'd most wanted to meet. Should she stand up and introduce herself? The dark woman might not like that. "Who is the woman?"

Joseph tugged at her sleeve. "Come on. She is one of the pastor's slaves. I know not her name. Let us go, Verity, before we are discovered."

She pulled her sleeve free. "I would like to meet the girls."

Joseph came back to her side. "They are from the village. They will not welcome you or me. We are the orphans, the ragpickers. The likes of them associate not with the likes of us."

Verity shook her head. "I am not a ragpicker. Not yet. I have only gone out the one day. One day cannot make me a ragpicker." She searched his face for the truth. "Can it?"

His blue eyes filled with something Verity didn't like, but she didn't have a name for it. It wasn't mean. It wasn't hurtful. But it was a type of hurting, and it was for her. She shook her head to stop him from saying the words out loud.

But he spoke anyway. "You are a ragpicker. There is nothing else for you here in the village, as there is nothing else for Becky or me until we are older. I will be old enough to apprentice next year, and Becky old enough to marry a couple more years after that."

"And me?" The words slipped out even though she didn't want the answer spoken aloud.

Joseph seemed to understand that. He took Verity's hand and drew her back, leading her away from the girls. Leading her back to the widow's dirt-floored shack and a life she didn't want.

The basket was lined with the old cheese rags for the little girl, then topped with a full wheel of cheese, and because it didn't seem enough, Hannah added a sack of their dried apple rings.

Her children loved them, and the orphans deserved a treat as well.

"If thee pack it any fuller, I shan't be able to carry it all the way to the village." Hannah Jr. peered over her shoulder.

"Never fear, 'tis not heavy at all." Hannah lifted it and handed it over. "And thank thee for delivering it to the Buffingtons."

"I am happy to. I need more gray thread from the general store. Why I bought black the other day when 'twas gray I was out of is beyond me. I was not thinking."

"Perhaps thy mind was on another matter?" Hannah made the comment into a question, giving her daughter a chance to explain if she desired.

A rosy hue flushed Hannah Jr, but she smiled sweetly, as she always did. "I was as anxious to see Robert as thee were."

The urge to ask if it was only Robert whom she was anxious to see trembled on Hannah's lips, but she refrained from asking. It was already late morning, and her daughters needed to get on their way. There would be another time to discuss whatever was causing Hannah Jr.'s absentmindedness.

"Tamson!" Hannah called up the staircase. "Hurry if thee are to walk with Hannah Jr."

Her younger daughter bounded down the stairs, bonnet askew.

"I am ready."

Hannah chuckled as she straightened the bonnet, then took a shawl from the peg by the door and tied it around the girl's shoulders. "Now thee are ready. Enjoy thy walk, but tarry not. I shall need thy help to bring in the laundry before supper."

Tamson sighed as only a girl her age could.

Hannah Jr. ushered her sister out the door. "We will hurry back."

Hannah watched from the window. Her two girls, twelve years apart in age, couldn't be more different one from the other. Hannah Jr. was tall and blonde and reserved. Tamson was more stout, dark-haired like her father, and had a more spontaneous nature. But each was precious to her. As would be the little orphan girl...

If only.

With a sigh that almost matched that of her youngest girl, Hannah turned back to her chores, thankful for all she had while still aching for what might have been if the village elders would only listen.

The sun streamed down and warmed Verity's head, but it didn't touch her heart. Cold with dread, she approached the first house.

Alone.

A knock on the shack's door early that morning had announced the arrival of a sturdy young man who introduced himself as the brewer's son, Benjamin Buffington. The widow had been very suspicious when he announced that his father had sent him to cut wood for her for the winter. So suspicious that she ordered Joseph to go with him and keep an eye on him.

Which left Verity on her own to do the begging.

She tried to remember everything Joseph had told her. She wasn't to go to the same house or business twice in the same week. She was to look sad and needy as much as possible, including smudging her hands and face with dirt. And she was to thank the goodwives before she left, even if they had nothing to give her that week, because it would make them more likely to save something for her in the future.

Hours had passed since she'd left the shack. Hours she'd spent in indecision and fear. It was nearly the noon hour, judging by the sun overhead. She couldn't put it off much longer, or she'd not get anything collected, and Joseph had warned her not to return empty-handed.

The widow wouldn't be pleased by that.

With her shawl bunched around her neck, she stooped and looked at the dirt but couldn't bring herself to pick it up, much less rub it on her skin. She felt dirty enough, having lived and slept in her only dress for days. She longed for a bath, but the widow didn't appear to own a washtub, much less a curtain to go behind for privacy. Verity scratched her upper arm and stood.

She hadn't gone to this house before. She did as Joseph had taught her, going around behind to the alley. She let herself into the tidy fenced yard and approached the back porch. A lanky red dog rose from the top step and barked at her.

Verity froze.

"What is the fuss?" A rotund woman in her middle years stepped onto the porch. "Ah, we have a visitor." She tugged the dog away from the steps and shooed it to the other side of the porch. "Pay him no mind. He has not a mean bone in his body. All bark and no bite."

The dog's tail swished from side to side, and it no longer barked, so Verity came forward.

"There you be. Come on." The woman waved her on. "You must be the new girl with Widow Scudder."

"I am." Verity climbed the steps.

The dog pushed its way around the woman and sniffed Verity.

"You can pet him. He will not harm you."

Unused to dogs, Verity held out her hand. A long pink tongue wrapped around her fingers, quick and warm and then back again. She giggled.

"Red likes you. Come on inside." The woman held the door open. "Are you here to collect rags then?"

Shame crawled over her as Verity dried her hand on her shawl. "I am."

There must have been something of her shame in her voice, because the woman sat and took her hands. "'Tis but for a season, my dear. Not forever. What is your name?"

"Verity Manton."

"I am Goodie Sibley. You are welcome here. I have a couple of rags set by. I did not allow my husband to burn them, knowing someone would come looking. Rest a moment while I fetch them." She rose and left the room, which smelled of cinnamon and yeast.

A bowl sat near the hearth, its mound covered with a clean cloth. Verity resisted the urge to peek beneath at the dough. She used to make bread that way for Uncle William. She'd been too young to do much cooking or baking with Momma, but he'd taught her how to make a simple loaf of bread. Her mouth watered at the memory of it.

"Here you are." Goodie Sibley bustled back into the room and pressed the rags into Verity's hand. "And I have something else for you too." The merriment in her voice coaxed a smile from Verity that widened when the woman pulled a cloth from a plate on the table. "Take one." She held the plate for Verity.

Verity stuffed the rags in her pocket, and then lifted a cinnamon-coated scone and cradled it in her hand. Oh, how she wished her hands were clean, but dirty or not, she would lick every crumb from them.

"Would you like a cup of milk to wash that down?" Goodie Sibley gestured to a bench pulled up to the table. "Sit, and I will pour one."

It was on the tip of Verity's tongue to decline, but she hadn't tasted milk in a long time. The farmer who had delivered to Uncle William had stopped coming for fear of the fever, and the widow didn't appear to even own a milk jug at the shack. So Verity slipped onto the bench and sank her teeth into the scone, its sweetness melting on her tongue.

Far too soon, the treat was gone, the milk finished, and she was waving goodbye to the kind goodwife while petting Red's head. She hurried outside the fence and ducked behind the alley's hedges. Pulling the rags from her pocket, she smoothed them out. Two were old pieces of toweling with too many holes to be useful. One was the bottom of a stocking that had worn out. No doubt Goodie Sibley was knitting a replacement in the evenings.

Would three rags be enough to please the widow? Did this mean she needn't beg anymore for the day? The pieces of toweling were quite large despite the holes. It would take her and Becky hours and hours to unravel them into threads and then untwist the threads into fibers the papermaker would purchase.

What would Verity do to fill her hours before returning to the shack? Joseph had warned her not to return too soon, or the widow would just send her out again.

Voices reached her, and laughter. Verity peeked from behind the hedges.

Walking down the road came a young woman and a girl. The woman carried a large basket, and the girl—older than Verity—skipped along, chattering and laughing.

The scene drew Verity out of her hiding place before she'd realized it.

"Look." The girl pointed at Verity.

Verity froze, as she had with the dog. He'd turned out to be friendly, though, and friendship was something she craved. It gave her the courage to stand firm.

The young woman waved at her and headed in her direction. "Hello. I do not believe we have met." She stopped in front of Verity. They were dressed all in gray and white, but their clothing wasn't ragged or ill-fitting. "I am Hannah, but they call me Hannah Jr. because my mother has the same name."

"I am her sister, Tamson." The girl giggled. "They call me Tamson, no junior, because I am the first one in the family."

"Be not so silly," Hannah Jr. chided her. "Thee are named after our grandmother, Thomasine, whose nickname was Tamson." She turned back to Verity. "What is thy name?"

"Verity Manton."

"'Tis a pleasure to meet thee, Verity," Hannah Jr. said.

"Why do you say *thee*?" The question slipped out before Verity could consider if it was rude or not.

"Because we are Friends, and 'tis how we talk," Tamson said.

Friends? Verity perked at the word. "I would like to be your friend," she said.

Tamson clapped her hands. "Then thee shall! Hannah Jr., let us share some cheese and apple rings with Verity."

"Oh." The young woman glanced at her sister, brows drawn down. "But Mother said—"

"She packed more than enough. Thee know she did."

Verity relaxed when Hannah Jr. pulled back the covering of the basket, which exposed a whole wheel of cheese sliced into thin wedges. "Tamson is right. We would love to share with thee, Verity." She held the basket out. "Help thyself."

But Verity's hands were dirty, and she didn't wish to soil anything. "My hands are not clean."

Hannah Jr. pulled the basket back and lifted out two wedges, handing them over. "Mine are. Are two enough?"

One for her and one for Joseph, but what about Becky? The older girl had not warmed to Verity. Maybe a piece of cheese would help. "May I have three?"

"Of course." Hannah Jr. handed her another one, then dug three dried apple rings from a small sack and put them in Verity's hand.

"Hannah Jr. makes the cheese," Tamson said. "She is going to start teaching me next spring when the cows' milk is the best for cheese. I already help with the pressing and wrapping."

Verity knew nothing about making cheese, but she nodded politely as she slipped the wedges and rings into her pocket.

"We have to deliver this basket for our mother or we would stay and visit with thee. Perhaps we will see thee when next we come to town." Hannah Jr. covered the basket again.

"I hope so." Something for Verity to look forward to, like the bright spot on the horizon that flared before the sunrise.

"Where do thee live?" Tamson asked, but her sister shushed her and hurried her along to wherever they were going.

Verity was glad. She didn't want her new friends to know that she was a ragpicker living with the widow. Although, from the softness in Hannah Jr.'s eyes as she'd quieted Tamson, she understood.

But she'd offered her friendship to Verity anyway. If she would, maybe the reverend's daughter would too. Another bright spot that lightened Verity's heart.

Chapter 7

V ERITY SKIRTED THE VILLAGE after leaving the girls and walked along the forest edge, still too fearful to enter it alone. She followed the treeline until the *thwack* of an ax reached her. Gathering her shawl tightly to her shoulders as if it held more courage, she stepped into the trees, following the sound. It led her to Joseph and Benjamin.

In spite of the chill, both were stripped to their shirtsleeves, coats hung over a nearby bush. The brewer's son lifted a double-bit ax high above his head and drove it into the cut section of log at his feet. *Thwack!* The piece of log split into two, right down the middle.

"Someday, I will have muscles like that." Joseph set aside the saw he'd been using to cut small limbs from a downed tree and wiped his brow.

"Hefting kegs and barrels of ale and cider in Pa's shop builds muscles." He flexed an arm. "Perhaps you could apprentice with him when you are older."

"Do you think so?" Joseph dusted his hands off on the back of his breeches. "I would like that. Very much. I shall turn twelve come spring."

That soon? Verity would lose him then.

She rushed to his side. "You cannot leave in the spring."

"Whyever not?" He looked down his nose at her.

She turned her head away from Benjamin and dropped her voice to a whisper. "Because... because that would leave me all alone with the widow and Becky. And then what would I do?"

"Listen." He bent close to her ear. "By then you will be settled with the widow and used to being here. You will not need me to show you how to get on."

"But—"

"I will be too old to be a beggar and will need to work. Some boys are already apprenticed at my age, at least in Salem Town. Here in the village, the elders set the age at twelve."

Verity pressed her trembling lips together. "I do not want you to go away."

"'Twould not be away. 'Twould be just up the road." He sighed and put an arm around her shoulders before addressing Benjamin. "I shall return in a little while." He tipped his head toward Verity.

"I could use a break anyway." Benjamin stretched his arms over his head and rotated his neck.

Joseph led Verity to a path that looked familiar, and she clung to his hand until she recognized the split pine tree.

"Are we going to the cave?"

"We can talk there, and eat some of the nuts." He smiled at her. "Cutting wood made me hungry."

"Oh." Verity reached into her pocket. "I have some food two girls gave me." She slipped into the cave ahead of Joseph.

"What girls?" he asked.

"Their names were Hannah Jr. and Tamson. I have never heard of anyone named Tamson before, have you?"

"Nay. But I had never heard of anyone named Verity before either."

"Here is what they gave me." She withdrew the cheese and apple rings.

Joseph's eyes popped wide. "Why did you not eat it?"

"I wanted to share with you and Becky."

"That is not a good idea." He shook his head hard enough to mess his already tangled hair. "Becky would only tell the widow, and then she would not feed us dinner."

"Why would Becky do that?"

"To win favor with the old woman." He took one of the cheese slices and bit into it. "I cannot remember the last time I tasted cheese."

Verity bit into another one. It was delicious, both creamy and sharp. She licked her lips, then handed Joseph the last piece of cheese. "You can have it. Goodie Sibley let me eat a scone at her house earlier."

He grinned at her and took the cheese. "I knew you would do well begging. Pretty as you are, folks will want to give you things." He wolfed down the cheese and then shook a finger at her. "But that is why you cannot trust Becky. She used to be pretty, not like you, but small and pretty. Now..." He shrugged. "She is not."

Becky wasn't ugly. She needed a bath and to have her hair and clothing washed, but she was not uncomely. "Maybe if she smiled once in a while, she would not seem so..." Verity couldn't find the right word.

"Disagreeable?"

That word summed it up. "I think she is just unhappy."

"When you are little, you can be unhappy and get a lot of sympathy. But when you get to be Becky's age, you cannot."

"How old is she?"

"Two years older than me, so thirteen."

"How long has she been with the widow?"

"Since before I came."

How disagreeable would Verity be in the years to come, living in a dirty shack with the widow? Especially with Joseph gone.

"I do not want you to leave me with the widow. I do not want to become like Becky."

"Then we shall have to think of something for you to do other than collecting rags."

"Oh." She reached into her pocket and pulled out the rags Goodie Sibley had given her. "Will this be enough for today?"

Joseph grinned at her. "Well done! The widow will be pleased. Are you going to eat those apple rings?"

She handed him two and bit into the last one. It was sweet and chewy.

"You know." Joseph looked around the cave. "You could hide one of the towels in here and save it for a day when you do not collect as much."

"Would that not upset the widow?"

"We would not tell her, of course. But on days you collect more than you must, you can store them here, then retrieve them on days when you do not collect anything."

"What happens if nobody has any rags for me?"

"The widow is a firm believer in work for food. If you do not do the work to her satisfaction, she will not feed you." He leaned toward her, his expression earnest. "That is why you must eat whatever the goodwives give you. You cannot count on the widow. Sometimes, even if we all work hard, there is not enough food."

"I will share what I get with you."

"I will share what I have with you as well. But we will save the nuts for another day, since we had cheese and apples." He rose. "Hand me a towel, and then I best be getting back to help Benjamin with the wood."

"Can I come with you? I can stack the split wood."

"Sure." He tied the towel to the same root as the sack of nuts. "'Twill keep some varmint from stealing it for its winter den."

Verity followed him, making an effort to remember the landmarks around them past the split pine. There was a pair of large rocks at one point, and a clump of paperbark birch trees that leaned over the path in another. By the time they reached Benjamin, she was almost certain she could find the cave again on her own.

In case the day came when Joseph was gone.

Sunday arrived with a cold drizzle blanketing the countryside, so after meeting, Hannah and the ladies gathered in a corner inside the meetinghouse.

"Hannah Jr. and Tamson delivered a basket to Sarah Buffington on Monday. On the way there, they met the new girl. Her name is Verity."

"Such a pretty name," said Hester, and several of the other ladies agreed.

"Did anyone make a contact among the Puritans this week to help us?" Hannah asked before they got too far off track.

Two of the ladies who lived closest to town had been successful. Those living on farms farther out had not had the opportunity yet. All remained committed to do what they could.

"At the very least, we can toss our rags in the community dump. I hear the children often go there and search," said Isobel.

"That is a fine idea," Hannah agreed. "Is there anything else we should discuss?"

"I think so." Hester's voice was hesitant. "I came across something disturbing this week."

"Do tell us," Isobel said.

"I was in the forest cutting willow twigs to strip for the bark. I heard a voice, and then the voices of children. When I found them, it was the Puritan pastor's slave—I do not know her name—and the pastor's daughter and niece, Betty and Abigail. I met them once before in the mercantile."

Many people cut through the forest, or went in search of wild herbs and nuts. Hannah had done so herself many times. But that wouldn't have alarmed Hester. "What were they doing?"

"The slave woman was telling them a story. But 'twas not the kind of story someone should tell to children." Hester lowered her voice. "'Twas a story about evil things, like spirits and demons."

A collective gasp went up. Several of the men who had gathered across the building looked their way, including Caleb. Hannah met his glance and shook her head. She'd tell him later.

"I have always heard that the Puritans preach long and loud against such things." Isobel found her voice first. "I cannot believe their preacher would approve."

"Likely 'tis why the woman had taken the girls into the forest." Hester glanced around. "They did not see me, I am sure of that, but I"—she pressed her hand to her chest—"I felt something out there. Something very disquieting."

A chill wormed its way across Hannah's shoulders. "We should pass this along to our husbands and caution our children. 'Tis a foolish thing to stir up evil in our midst." Even more foolish if the Puritans found a way to attribute it to the Friends.

"I believe we can all agree on that," Isobel said.

They hurried to their wagons and carts, for the drizzle had picked up to a steadier rain. Caleb had put the cover on their wagon, so Hannah sat in the back with the children. Should she discuss what she'd learned in front of them? Or wait to speak with Caleb alone?

"What caused the women to be upset after the meeting?" Caleb asked.

Perhaps that was her answer, best to speak of it. After all, the children might come across those girls in the forest at another time. She related all that she'd heard.

"This is very grave." Caleb stopped at the brewer's and turned sideways on the wagon's bench so he could see the children. "Playing with evil is dangerous."

"But 'twas just a story," Tamson said.

Robert stood to leave the wagon.

"Sit down, son." Caleb set the brake on the wagon and turned back to the children. "'Tis important that thee understand this. Stories are powerful ways to teach people, and not just children. Jesus taught in parables, which was what they called stories in that time."

Even little Jonathan listened intently, quiet in Hannah Jr.'s arms.

"A well-told story will carry on down through the generations from father to son, from mother to daughter. Never think that something is 'just a story.' I am not chiding Tamson." He smiled at their daughter. "There are many adults who understand not the power of story. We must be careful what we allow into our homes, our heads, and our hearts. If we open the doors of any of those to evil, 'tis the same as inviting it in."

"Do thee think the slave woman is evil?" Robert asked.

"I know nothing of her, so I could not say." Caleb glanced at Hannah.

"Nor do I," Hannah said.

Caleb Jr. glanced around the family, then focused on his father. "There are things said about the slaves who come from the islands."

"I have heard the rumors." Caleb appeared to be choosing his words with care. "But rumors are not facts, so we should not repeat them, nor expound on things we know not of. The point is, we"—he drew a circle with his finger incorporating the whole family—"do not invite evil into our house, or our heads, or our hearts. These belong to the Lord only. Am I understood?"

The children nodded, only Tamson seeming a little alarmed. Hannah would need to draw that one aside for a long talk at some point.

With a wave goodbye, Robert jumped off the back of the wagon.

Caleb started the wagon toward home. The forest bordered the road, and for the first time since the Indian uprising years ago, dread of what it might conceal niggled at Hannah. Had there been an invitation to evil happening in these very woods so close to their home? Surely, the pastor would correct his daughter as Caleb had corrected theirs.

Would he not?

Chapter 8

V ERITY HAD ASKED JOSEPH how long she'd been at the widow's, because without going to church on Sundays, she couldn't keep track of the weeks. He'd said a month, but it felt like so much longer.

The leaves were all gone now. A fresh dusting of snow covered the frozen ground and hid objects in the village dump. It chilled her fingers and nose. Her toes, which threatened to push through the front of her too-tight shoes, were numb for most of the day.

She didn't cry herself to sleep anymore, but she still missed Uncle William and thought of him often. He wouldn't be happy that she was sent out to beg every day. He wouldn't be happy that she was hungry, which happened mostly on Sundays. During the week, the goodwives of the village gave her bread, cheese, dried fruit, and sometimes a cup of milk or a piece of ham.

Too many of them recently, however, had no rags to offer her. So this morning, again, she was pawing through the contents of the village dump, hoping to find anything to satisfy the widow. She'd done as Joseph said and kept back rags in the cave, but this week, she'd had to use them all. And still she'd collected nothing but food from the goodwives. Food she no longer felt guilty for eating or sharing just with Joseph.

If only she could find a scrap of cloth and maybe a button. She'd found a button once, and the widow had been so pleased. The old woman hadn't sold it, however. She'd sewn it on her coat, which had been without any buttons at all. At least the widow had a coat. Verity pulled her shawl closer, ignoring its sour smell in order to gain more warmth.

Verity tugged on a piece of broken board, but it was frozen into the ground. She gave it another tug and yelped when a splinter bit into her palm. Blood dotted her skin, drawing tears that grew icy on her cheeks. What was she going to do? She'd been to every house in the village this week. Every one except for the scary house from which Joseph had warned her to stay away. The Goods' house.

She wiped the blood on her skirt, where it blended into the stains already there, then she started back toward the village. Her stomach rumbled. Perhaps the woman at the scary house would give her something to eat, if nothing else.

What other choice did she have?

Working her way down the alley, her steps slowed. Joseph wasn't afraid of anything, but he'd warned her away from this house. Fear made her legs wobble, but hunger kept her moving forward.

The house came into view, standing unkempt and almost bare of whitewash. The back porch steps sagged. Would they even hold her slight weight? There was no fence, so no need to open a gate, nothing to stop her from approaching.

Except the dread that filled her.

Her stomach rumbled again, pinching inside. Between the fear and the hunger, hunger was winning.

A piece of curtain, the bottom missing, moved at the window as Verity reached the first step. She counted each one as she climbed, then she pulled in a long breath and held it as she tapped on the door. Nothing happened. She tapped again. A dog barked inside, followed by a yip and a curse in a deep voice. Before Verity could flee, the door swung open and an unshaven man filled the opening.

"What do you want?"

"Please, sir." Verity didn't recognize the squeak of her own voice. "Do you have a rag to spare, or a crust of bread?"

"Go away, you little beggar. You will get nothing here." He started to close the door, but a half-grown pup came up beside him and barked. He kicked the animal onto the porch. "That goes for you too. Get out of here."

The pup landed in a whimpering heap at Verity's feet as the door slammed shut.

"You poor thing." Fear for herself was replaced by the need to comfort the animal. She wrapped her arms around it, and its pink tongue washed her face. "You must come with me," she whispered into its red-and-white fur. "'Tis not safe for you here."

When she hurried down the steps, the pup was at her side. What was she going to do with it? The widow would never allow a dog at the shack. She could barely feed the four of them. But Verity couldn't see the poor animal go back to that house, where the man had abused it. And besides, he'd ordered it away. He didn't want the dog.

Maybe because it'd been mistreated, or maybe because it was unwanted, but for whatever reason, the pup needed her. And Verity was suddenly determined to take care of it. Somehow.

She headed for the only safe place she could think of. Joseph's cave.

A walk to the village with her daughter was something to enjoy on a normal day. Hannah Jr. was free from working in the dairy, and Hannah had another basket of rags and cheese to share with Sarah Buffington. She was anxious to know if the first basket had been accepted by the widow for the orphans. But there was that issue she couldn't avoid any longer, and with just the two of them, it was the right opportunity. Hannah took a deep breath of the frosty air and plunged into the topic she'd been avoiding for too long.

"'Tis time, I think, for us to discuss thy future."

Hannah Jr. stiffened beside her without pausing her stride. "I am very happy in the dairy. 'Twould be fine by me to keep things as they are."

"For how long?" She glanced at her daughter, who kept her face forward, looking down the road. "Do thee not want a family of thy own? A husband and children?"

"Are thee desiring grandchildren already?"

Hannah heard the attempt to change the subject, but if she pulled back now, they might never have this discussion. And every mother's instinct in her was on edge.

"Grandchildren would be a blessing, of course, but I would see thee settled at some point. I was married and had thee on the way by the time I was thy age."

A sigh that was more of a huff whitened the air in front of her daughter. "I know. But thee had Father, and I have not found anyone like him yet."

"He is special, thee will get no argument from me on that, but has there been no young man to catch thy eye from our community?"

"Nay. If there were, thee would know it." Hannah Jr. looked at her then, her eyes almost pleading for her to stop asking questions.

"And the young Puritan men of the village." She needed to ask. "Has one of them caught thy eye?" She braced herself for the answer.

It didn't come right away, which was answer enough, but Hannah kept walking. Kept waiting. Her daughter would not lie to her. She would answer when she was ready.

They'd nearly reached the village when Hannah Jr. stopped and faced her. "Will Father be sorely disappointed in me?"

It was one thing to suspect the truth, and another to hear it confirmed. "So thee are drawn to one of the Puritan young men?"

Hannah Jr. dipped her chin.

"Will thee tell me which one?" Although she had a pretty good idea it would come down to two—the brewer's twin sons, who were three years younger than her daughter, which should buy them all some time.

The name came like a whisper on the wind. "Benjamin Buffington."

If her daughter indeed married him at some point, they'd have two Benjamins in the family once Benji outgrew his childish nickname. But then, they had two Calebs and two Hannahs, so that wasn't an issue, just a random thought to put off the more difficult one.

"A Puritan."

"I know, Mother." Hannah Jr.'s voice was filled with pain. "I did not wish this, truly I did not. But neither can I think of marrying another when he is the one who fills my thoughts. 'Twould not be right or fair to another man."

Of course it wouldn't.

"I would rather remain a spinster in the dairy, if thee and Father will allow me to stay."

"Allow thee?" Hannah pulled her daughter into her arms. "'Tis thy home, now and for as long as thee wishes."

"And Father?" The words were muffled against Hannah's hair.

"I will speak with him." She pushed Hannah Jr. out to arm's length and studied her lovely face, creased with worry lines.

"Know this, he loves thee fiercely. He wants only the best for thee and all our children."

"I know." The stiffness eased from her shoulders.

"Have thee...?" How best to word this? "Have thee made any promises to Benjamin? Or he any to thee?"

"Nay. We have barely spoken but a handful of times."

And yet, her regard for the young man was deep, and Hannah suspected it had been growing for some time. Did the young man feel the same? Where would such an unlikely pairing lead them? Not that intermarriages between the faiths were unheard of, but they were uncommon and filled with difficulties. Puritans at best tolerated the Friends. And at worst—but Hannah couldn't let those dark thoughts cloud her at this moment.

Hannah Jr. shifted away from her. "Mother, look. The little ragpicker girl, Verity."

Hurrying toward them was the girl, head down, determination in her limping stride. A dog trotted at her heels.

"Verity?" Hannah Jr. called when she was close enough.

The girl startled, jerking up her head. She looked around warily.

"'Tis only us. We did not mean to frighten thee," Hannah Jr. said in a most soothing voice.

Recognition flickered in the girl's expression. "Hannah Jr.?"

"Aye. Thee remembered." Her daughter sounded pleased. "But who is that following thee?"

Verity glanced down at the dog that had stopped beside her and was licking her fingers. If he was going to be her dog, he must have a name. It should be something special so he knew he was loved. Because even though he'd been kicked to her by that awful man, she already loved him. She knelt and wrapped her arms around his furry neck, giving him the first name that popped into her head. "This is Button."

Hannah Jr. pointed to the older woman beside her. "This is my mother, Hannah."

Verity rose and bobbed a curtsy.

"Nay, child," Hannah said. "Thee have no need to show me such deference. We Friends believe all are equal in the sight of God."

"You are a friend too?" Verity released Button and came closer.

"Aye. And I have something for thee." She pushed the cloth covering her basket to the side and reached in, but paused. "Are thee hungry?"

"I am."

Hannah withdrew several slices of cheese. The same kind of cheese Hannah Jr. had given her before. Verity's mouth watered.

Button whined at her feet.

Hannah withdrew two more slices. "'Twould seem that Button is hungry too."

Verity forced herself to accept them slowly, not snatch them from her hand. She slipped the slices into her pocket, the worry about what to feed Button eased.

The kind lady reached back into the basket and pulled out two small rounds of bread. "Have thee room in thy pocket for these?"

"Aye. Thank you." She held the pocket open, and Hannah added the rounds.

"One more thing." Hannah pulled out a length of cloth and handed it to her. "I understand thee collect rags for Widow Scudder. Perhaps thee can make use of this old blanket." She wrapped it around Verity's shoulders.

What a wonderful blessing it was to have friends. Tears stung the backs of Verity's eyes, but this time, they weren't all sad tears. Some were happy ones.

"Why are thee limping?" Hannah Jr. asked. "Did thee fall or have an accident?"

Shame crept over her that her new friend had to ask such a question. She stared at the toes of her shoes.

The older Hannah knelt beside her, one hand rubbing Button's ears. "What makes thee hurt?"

"My shoes are too small." Then the whole story came pouring out of her. How Uncle William had died before he could buy her new shoes, the funeral, the widow, her belongings taken away, and how much she wished for a bath. She wasn't even sure she made any sense. The words tumbled out in a flurry, chased by emotions she'd kept tightly controlled for weeks.

Before she knew it, she was in the older woman's arms, sobbing, while Button washed the side of her face he could reach. She should let go and be on her way to the cave, but it felt so good to have a pair of adult arms around her again, and a soft body to lean against. With her eyes closed, she could almost imagine her mother holding her.

Gentle fingers smoothed the hair away from Verity's face. "I believe we still have a pair or two of Tamson's old shoes at the farm. Would thee like to come and try them on to see if they fit?"

Verity opened her eyes. It wasn't her mother, it was the elder Hannah, but the softness in her eyes drew Verity like a moth to a lantern. "Aye."

"'Tis a bit of a walk," Hannah Jr. said, "but we could take turns carrying thee and take the pressure off thy poor feet."

Such kindness almost sent her into another flood of tears, but Verity managed a nod.

"Our farm is north of town along this road. 'Tis easy to find from the widow's."

They mostly live on the north side of town, farmers, so they are easy to avoid.

Joseph's warning about the Quakers rang in her ears. "I cannot go north of town."

"Why can thee not?" Hannah Jr. asked.

"Because of the Quakers." Verity couldn't stop the shudder that shook her. "They live there. Joseph told me that even the widow fears them."

"Verity." Hannah Jr. knelt beside her. "Mother and I are two of those the Puritans call Quakers. As is Tamson. Thee have met us. Surely thee do not believe we mean thee any harm."

Quakers.

Fear shot through her, and Verity stumbled in her hurry to back away from them. Button whined at her side. Then she was running, her toes nearly breaking against the tight leather, Button barking and running beside her.

Without a thought of the darkness or Indians, she plunged into the forest.

Chapter 9

N IGHT WAS APPROACHING. THE trees closed in on Verity and Button. A cold wind rattled the bare branches overhead.

In her terror, Verity had entered the forest in an area she didn't know. She'd run until she'd fallen in a heap, her feet unable to support her any longer. The pup had snuggled close, and she'd wrapped them both in the blanket.

Where was she?

How long had she slept?

Would Joseph come looking for her?

The emotions of the day broke over her again. Despair at not collecting any rags, compassion for the pup kicked to her feet, joy at meeting friends on the road who had given her food and comfort, and then the terror of realizing they were Quakers—the people who frightened even Widow Scudder.

Verity sat up, and Button whined, pawing at her pocket that had been beneath her while she slept. He must be hungry. She fished out two slices of cheese and gave one to Button. It tasted as good as she'd remembered and was gone far too soon. She took a round of bread and broke it in half, sharing it with her dog. He licked his lips and stared at her.

"'Tis enough for now." She rose and brushed off her dirty dress, then shook out her shawl and blanket before wrapping them around her again, glad for the double layer of warmth. "We have to find the cave before it gets any darker. I cannot take you to the widow's shack. She would never let me keep you."

She started off, Button by her side. When she should be terrified, lost and alone in the forest with darkness settling in, the red-and-white pup's quiet confidence gave her courage. They stopped at a spring and drank their fill, then moved on until a familiar clump of paperbark birch came into view.

"There." She pointed them out to Button. "I know where we are now." She hobbled as fast as her sore feet would allow and found the path that led to the cave. They arrived as the last of the sun's rays seeped from between the trees and plunged them into the gloom of a forest at night.

Verity sat with her back against the rough wall where she could look up through the hole and see stars. Their feeble light was better than none at all. She folded her hands like she'd been taught to pray. "Lord God, I need help."

She peeked between her lashes at Button, who watched her with his head cocked, red ears perked, tail swishing against the dirt floor.

She squinched her eyes shut. "And Button needs help too. I cannot return to the shack tonight. There might be Indians in the forest." Fear caused her voice to wobble, but surely God could still hear her. "And Button cannot go to the shack at all. The widow would not like that. He will starve if I cannot sneak him enough food. Please help us, Lord God."

She opened her eyes and patted the ground beside her. When Button snuggled close, she wrapped them both in the blanket. What would Uncle William have thought of her sitting in a cave, cuddled with a dog? He'd not had a dog while she lived with him, nor had her parents that she remembered. But Button's soft fur and warmth comforted her, and his steady breathing combated the cave's silence. It all combined to make her very sleepy.

The next thing she knew, Button was growling beside her. He'd risen from the blanket, legs rigid, head low, the white hair on his neck spiking, almost glowing in the starlight.

"What is it?" she whispered.

Button pounced on something that issued a shrill squeak. It was cut off by the crunch of teeth against bone. Button turned around with his head up. It was too dark to see clearly, but what looked to be a rat's tail hung from his mouth.

"Oh!" Verity pulled the blanket tighter around her. Before she could think of what to do, Button was eating the rat.

"You should not eat that evil thing." Her stomach cramped at the thought.

They'd had a cat in Maine, with gray stripes and yellow eyes. She'd caught and eaten rats, mice, chipmunks, and even small rabbits on occasion. Papa had said that God fed her better than they could.

That was before the Indians.

Was God feeding Button now?

She looked up through the hole to the stars beyond. Would God feed her too?

The Quaker women had. They'd given her the blanket and offered her shoes.

Yet... they were evil. Everyone said so. Even Joseph, and he seemed to know everyone and everything. But thinking back on the day, and on meeting Hannah Jr. and Tamson before, they hadn't seemed evil at all. They'd seemed... very nice.

Had God sent the Quakers to her to give her food and shoes? After all, God sent the rat to feed Button, and rats were evil.

Maybe the Quakers weren't evil at all.

The cold seeped through her blanket and shawl. "Come here, Button." She lifted the blanket's edge, and the pup cuddled against her again, licking his lips.

Verity was too tired to think anymore. Tomorrow, she'd have to decide what to do. Resting easy that Button would keep any other vermin away, she drifted back to sleep thinking about the Quakers' cheese and shoes that wouldn't crush her toes.

"I should have gone after her." Hannah perched on the edge of their bed, braiding her hair for the night. "The poor child was so frightened."

"Chasing her would have frightened her even more, I should think." Caleb sat with pillows propped behind him, watching her. "Thee cannot undo the things she has been taught about us."

"Why can I not?" She faced him. "I can show her kindness. I can feed her, put shoes on her feet, give her a place to bathe, perhaps a clean dress to wear. The child needs care. Surely, she would come to see us as who we are, not who the Puritans say we are."

"My dear, she has probably been told from birth that we Friends are agents of the devil." Caleb raised his hand when she opened her mouth. "Thee know 'tis what they say of us."

"I will never understand how a people who profess to adhere to the Bible and God's laws can so willingly tell such falsehoods."

"Because they are blinded by their own perceived righteousness." He glanced out the window before meeting her eyes again. "I think it may be more than that, however."

Hannah waited. When Caleb was thinking deeply, he needed time to bring forth the words. She'd learned long ago to listen when he did. Her husband was a man of God, one who believed with all his heart, and one who would ponder and search the proper godly response to any situation. She loved that about him.

Even if sometimes she'd rather rant and rave against a situation herself—like now.

"Our Puritan neighbors try so hard not to sin. They instill the fear of sinning in their children from a very young age. But perhaps 'tis not the most healthy type of fear."

She drew her legs onto the bed and faced him squarely. "We have taught our children not to sin, even though we know they will fall short at times."

"Aye, we have taught them not to sin, but we have not instilled in them a *fear* of sin." He rubbed his chin, another endearing way he had of delaying his response as he thought. "As thee said, we know our children will fall short at times, as do we. If they were fearful of that, terrified of it, it could hinder their ability to lead good and fruitful lives. Do thee see?"

"So afraid to sin that they also fear to try something difficult?"

"Or something new. Like we Friends—in person and not just in thought—are new to the young girl."

Could he be correct? "If she has been taught that we are a sinful people, then her fear of us comes from a very deep place, from the fear of sinning itself more than the fear of us as a people."

"What a wonderfully intelligent woman I share my bed with." The look he gave her was filled with love, admiration, and that special something that existed just between them.

"Thee are a wise man, my husband." She pulled back the covers and slid in beside him. "But if that is the case, how is it that the pastor's own daughter and niece have been found in the forest listening to evil stories from the slave woman? Surely, they would know the sinfulness of that."

"Thee remember the parable of the prodigal son?"

"They are but children, no older than Tamson. They are too young to be prodigals."

"Perhaps. But not too young to be drawn to what is forbidden." He bumped his shoulder against hers. "As our Benji demonstrated with thy cookie jar yesterday."

The little scamp had raided her store of cookies, and not for the first time. Of all her children, he was the one who craved sweets, and cookies in particular. "I corrected him, of course."

"Thee did not make him fearful, however. Thy correction was loving and understanding yet firm. He knew of thy displeasure at his actions. I believe that is in keeping with the Lord's correction in our lives if we listen to Him and change our ways."

"Well, Benji is in a growth spurt. I will pay attention that he eats enough at mealtimes. And I need to sew him new breeches. Those I have left from Caleb Jr. and Robert are little more than rags."

Which brought her back to thinking about Verity.

Caleb yawned and slid down until his head was on the pillow. "Sleep, wife. Tomorrow is soon enough to plot and plan how thee can once again meet up with the ragpicker and take her Tamson's old shoes."

"How do thee know that is what I was thinking?"

"Twenty-three years of marriage." His voice rumbled in her ear as she stretched out beside him. His arm came around her, solid and warm and comforting.

What comfort had little Verity found this night? *Lord God, please watch out for her.*

"Verity!" Joseph's voice reached through the fog of her sleep. "Verity, are you out here?"

Button growled but didn't move from under the blanket.

Verity sat and rubbed her eyes, the glow of morning shining through the hole above her. "Joseph?" She raised her voice. "I am here."

He filled the cave's low opening. "What happened? Why did you not return to—" His mouth dropped open when Button raised his head from the blanket. "What is this?"

"His name is Button." Verity hugged the dog. "He is my dog now."

"Nay. The widow will never allow it." Sorrow filled his voice. "She would order me to kill him if you took him to the shack."

"Then I cannot go back." The words burst from her before she could think about them.

"But you cannot stay here." He spread his arms, taking in the cave's interior.

"Why can I not?" Her stomach growled.

He pointed at her belly. "That is one reason. Another is the weather. Soon the snow will come and you would freeze to death, the pup too."

"I will not let him freeze. And God has already fed him."

Joseph settled back on his heels. "What?"

"God sent a rat last night. Button killed and ate it."

"Lucky for you, or the rat might have bitten you."

That hadn't occurred to Verity, and she didn't like the thought at all. Button had protected her, though, and now she must protect him.

"Are you not afraid of the dark and Indians?"

"I am." She rubbed Button's head. "Button will protect me, as he did from the rat."

"That pup"—Joseph pointed at Button and got his finger licked—"could not stop an Indian."

She lifted her chin. "You told me there were no Indians in this forest."

He slumped against the wall. "I have never seen any, but 'tis not impossible that some might pass through."

His admission sent a tremor through her, and Button pressed closer. "I did not collect any rags yesterday, even though I went to the scary house."

"You did?" Surprise raised Joseph's brows and voice. "You went to the Goods' house?"

She told him the whole story, including about Hannah and Hannah Jr., and then wiped her tears on the blanket. "I want to see the Quaker women again."

Joseph sat upright. "Nay!"

"They were nice to me and to Button. Much nicer than the widow."

"But they are evil and will turn you away from God."

She curled her hands into fists and pounded her thighs, startling Button. "I do not believe that anymore."

"Verity!" The shock on her friend's face almost undid her newfound confidence.

"They were kind and clean and smelled nice." She reached into her pocket and pulled out the last three slightly mashed pieces of cheese, handing one to Joseph and giving another to Button, who wolfed his down. "They shared this with me."

Joseph stared at his piece of cheese as if it might be poison.

Verity bit into hers. "*Mmm*." She smacked her lips. "Just as good as the last they gave me. And bread too."

After watching her a moment longer, Joseph stuffed the cheese in his mouth.

"'Tis ever so good." She finished her piece and withdrew the bread, dividing it into thirds and passing it out. "Would someone evil make such good cheese and bread and give it out without asking for anything in return?"

"I know not." Joseph ate his portion of bread. "But the widow says they are evil." This time, there was less conviction in his tone.

"The widow does not even attend church, nor allow us to attend."

"My parents warned me of the Quakers. Did your parents or uncle not warn you?"

She couldn't remember her parents saying anything about Quakers, but there were plenty of Puritans in Salem Town who'd been willing to speak out against the Quakers in the church. Even Uncle William had commented on them sometimes. He'd never called them evil, but she'd gotten the impression that he didn't approve of their ways.

If he'd known that their ways were to give her food, comfort, and friendship, would he have thought differently?

She hoped so, because she was going to meet them again, whether Joseph helped her find their farm or not. She liked them—and she was pretty sure they wouldn't order Button to be killed.

Chapter 10

"A RE YOU SURE THIS is the right farm?" Peeking from behind a row of bramble bushes at the large house flanked by outbuildings, Verity gripped Joseph's sleeve.

There was a tall barn made of milled boards with a herd of brown cows behind it, and several log structures, including what must be a smokehouse from the plume of gray lingering at its top and the fragrant scent of smoldering hickory that reached them.

The two-story house was also made of milled boards and whitewashed until it gleamed in the midmorning sun. A line of washing hung to one side, white sheets dancing in the gentle breeze.

A door banged, and Tamson scurried from what looked to be the outhouse, sending a flock of chickens squawking as she ran through them and dashed up the steps into the house.

A black-and-white dog raised its head at her.

"Aye," Verity placed her hand on Button, who wriggled at the sight of another dog. "'Tis the right place. That was Tamson. I met her before on the road. She was with Hannah Jr.

They gave me the first cheese I shared with you." She turned to Joseph. "She is very nice."

Joseph studied the scene before them. "Nothing looks evil."

"Nothing at all. Not like the scary house in town where the mean man kicked Button." She rubbed the dog's head. "Not like the widow's shack either. Imagine having freshly washed sheets." Or any sheets at all. Verity's bed at the widow's was a wooden shelf attached to the wall and a scratchy blanket. No sheets. No pillow. No mattress.

"My mother used to hang out sheets." Joseph's voice was smaller than normal, so Verity took his hand and held it.

"Come with me."

He shook his head and took a step back.

"Please. At least until they answer the door?" For all her confidence of moments ago, she didn't want to approach the house alone. "They might give you something to eat." She and Joseph had argued in the cave for a long time before Joseph had agreed to show her where he thought the Quakers lived. That and the long walk had worn through their skimpy breakfast of shared cheese and bread.

His fingers tightened on hers. "If I see something wrong and tell you to run, you have to run. Do you agree?"

She couldn't run in her shoes, and with the ground frozen, she couldn't run without them. Not mentioning either problem, she nodded.

"Are you ready?"

Mouth too dry to speak, she nodded again.

They picked their way through the brambles, Joseph having to untangle her blanket from the thorns twice, while Button bounded out in front of them.

A pounding reached them, and Verity gripped Joseph's hand tighter. "What is that?"

"Someone hammering wood." He looked down at her. "That makes sense, because he is said to be a carpenter as well as a farmer."

"Oh." Her empty stomach seemed filled with butterflies, but Joseph led her on.

The dog on the porch rose and stood at attention, its ears pricked toward them, but it made no menacing sound. When they were halfway to the house, the door swung open and Tamson appeared on the porch with a large wicker basket. She stopped on the top step and shaded her eyes, looking straight toward them. "Verity? Is it thee?" She dropped the basket on the porch and hurried to them, the dog running beside her. "Who have thee brought with thee?"

The girl's open smile and honest face shooed away Verity's nerves. "This is my friend, Joseph, and my dog, Button."

"Welcome to our farm, all of you." She bent and scratched behind Button's ears while he sniffed noses with the black-and-white dog. "This is Rags. Rags, meet Button." She rose and grinned at them. "Come to the house. Mother will be so pleased to see thee."

"She will?"

"Mother was very distraught that thee ran from her yesterday. She worried about thee all evening, afraid thee would get lost in the forest."

"I did. But I found Joseph's cave and stayed there all night with Button."

"Thee poor thing." The older girl wrapped an arm around Verity's shoulder. "Come on. Thee must be hungry. Joseph too."

Verity held her ground and looked up at Tamson. "And Button?"

"Button can keep Rags company." The girl smiled, but Verity needed more.

"Your mother will not send Joseph out to kill Button, will she?"

Tamson looked stricken. "Mother would never kill a dog. She is uncommonly fond of them."

"She asks because Widow Scudder…" Joseph let this sentence trail off with a shrug.

"That horrid old woman." Tamson slapped her hand over her mouth. "I should not have said that. 'Tis not up to me to pass judgment on another. Mother and Father are forever reminding me of that." Tamson started for the house, Joseph on one side and Verity on the other.

All thoughts of evil fled. Hannah liked dogs, and she'd worried about Verity's safety.

Hannah was nothing like the widow, and that was good enough for Verity.

There was no sign of Tamson gathering sheets when Hannah glanced out the window. "Where did that girl go?"

Jonathan looked up at her from the floor, where he was busy banging a wooden spoon against a hollow block Caleb had given the boys. Benji helped by setting the blocks back into place when his little brother knocked them all down. It was noisy, but it kept them occupied while she washed potatoes for a pot of soup.

Benji rose and ran into the back room. "Ma! Come quick!"

Hannah dried her hands and reached the back room as the door swung open.

Tamson entered with Verity and a boy behind her who was close in age to Tamson. In the small entryway, the first thing she noticed was the odor. How long had it been since either child had bathed? She did her best not to wrinkle her nose. "Verity, what a wonderful surprise. Who is this thee have brought with thee?"

"Joseph." Verity clung to Tamson's hand. "He lives with Widow Scudder too. He is an orphan, like me." Her voice trailed off until it was barely a whisper on the last word.

Hannah's heart squeezed at the injustice of sending children to live with someone who could not properly care for them. They were undernourished, poorly clothed, and had a complete lack of hygiene. Hannah had the wild desire to find the village elders and slap one of them—if not all of them. They sorely tried her pacifist beliefs.

She'd need to repent of that later, but first, the children.

"I am so glad thee came and brought Joseph."

"And Button." Tamson pointed at the porch where the red-and-white pup sat with its tongue lolling out one side of his mouth in a canine grin. "May I bring him in, Mother?"

"Of course, if it is all right with Verity."

"Aye, mistress."

"My name is Hannah. We Friends—those thee know as Quakers—we use our given names only. I hope thee and Joseph will as well."

"Except I call her Mother, and the boys call her Ma." Tamson giggled.

Hannah ushered them into the kitchen, ignoring the smell. "Tamson, fetch the shoes thee outgrew that might fit Verity." She turned to their guests. "Are thee hungry? We shall have soup in a little while, but I have a pan of cornbread and fresh milk until then." There was no mistaking the gleam in Joseph's eyes, and Verity nodded.

She set them at the table, both Benji and Jonathan joining them, while she filled bowls with cornbread and poured milk over the top. She fixed another bowl and set it on the floor for the pup, ordering Rags to his corner of the kitchen since he'd already eaten that morning. All was quiet while they ate and she finished readying the potatoes for their soup.

Tamson returned with the shoes and some clothing. "Do thee think these will fit too?" She held up an old pair of

Robert's worn-out breeches that Hannah had intended to give to Verity for rags and a shirt in not much better condition. But, looking at the boy, they were better than what he wore. Tamson also held one of her outgrown dresses that was in much better shape than Verity's.

"Those will do nicely."

But though Joseph perked up, Verity looked stricken.

Hannah went to her and sat on the chair beside her. "What is wrong?"

"I am too dirty to put on those clean clothes."

Hannah's heart broke for the girl.

"Then thee must have a bath," Tamson said. "I will fetch the tub and ready it." She dropped the clothing on the table.

"Would thee like that, Verity?" Hannah asked.

Tears welled in the child's eyes, and she nodded.

"Finish thy cornbread. I shall heat the water."

"May I have a bath too?" Joseph looked down at the rags he wore. "I need one, too, before I put on clean clothes." Glancing up, he sent a troubled look at Verity. "What will the widow say if we come back wearing new clothes?"

"Perhaps she will be pleased when thee bring thy old clothes back to her for rags," Hannah said.

What sort of a woman put such fear in children?

Verity set her spoon down. "I do not wish to go back."

"Nor do I wish thee to." The words were out before Hannah could think about them. Caleb would support her, but what sort of a hornet's nest would this open with the village elders? She didn't care. The child—the children—needed her.

She busied herself with heating water while Tamson set up the copper bath and rigged the curtain in the corner near the hearth for privacy.

Button lifted his head from licking his bowl clean and barked.

"Hello." Hannah Jr. entered the kitchen. "I see we have visitors."

"And they are going to stay." Tamson had an armload of toweling and a huge grin on her face.

Hannah turned so the children couldn't see her face. *If only it could be that easy.*

The warm water was soothing, the soap smelling of lavender, and Verity would have stayed in the copper tub all day if she could have. But Joseph was waiting for his turn, and that lovely blue dress draped across a chair waited for her along with black shoes sporting brass buckles. Tamson had even brought Verity a clean shift and stockings.

How long had it been since she'd been clean? How long since Uncle William's funeral? She didn't know. She'd lost all track of the days—weeks—since arriving at the widow's. It was all like a very bad dream. In some ways, even worse than the dreams about Indians. Those dreams went away when she awoke. When she awoke at the widow's, she was still there.

She stood in the tub and let the water drip off her.

"Can I assist thee?" Tamson asked through the curtain.

"Aye." Uncle William hadn't assisted her with a bath. It wouldn't have been proper. But when Tamson slipped behind the curtain and helped towel Verity's hair dry, it brought a flood of memories of Momma doing the same thing.

"Thee have such pretty hair, and it wants to curl in the steam." Tamson leaned over and looked into Verity's eyes. "And the nicest blue-gray eyes."

The older girl's hair was straight as a needle and black as night, and her eyes were a dark shade of gray, with neither blue nor brown highlights.

"Your eyes are much prettier."

Tamson cocked her head. "Mine have no color at all."

"Hurry, girls," Hannah said from behind the curtain. "The men will be in for dinner soon, and Joseph would like to bathe first."

Tamson giggled as she helped Verity into the clean shift and dress, and even helped with the stockings. But Verity grabbed the shoes and slipped them on herself. Oh, the blessed comfort they offered, with room for each toe. She sighed, then scurried out of Joseph's way.

"Why, Verity," Hannah Jr. said, "thee look fit to attend meeting."

"Meeting?" Who would she be meeting?

"'Tis what we Friends call our church," Tamson said. "Mother, may I take Verity up to my room?"

Hannah gave her daughter a pointed look. "Do not get too far ahead of things. We must speak with thy father first."

Tamson nodded, then pulled Verity along behind her, Button and Rags following.

"Mother has to say that, but I know Father. He will agree to thee staying with us." She grinned at Verity. "'Twill be like having a younger sister. Thee can share my bed."

A younger sister? Another memory came back, one of Verity hugging her younger sister close at night, cuddled under one of Momma's quilts to keep warm.

They entered a small room on the second floor with a window looking out at the tall barn with the cows behind. The window was shut against the cold, but Verity could imagine it open with a cool breeze and the smells of the farm drifting in during the summer months.

Now, however, with it closed, the room smelled of cedar. Covered with a patchwork quilt, the bed took up most of the space. Its dark red, carved wooden posts reached for the ceiling. A matching chest rested at the foot of the bed. One wall had pegs where Tamson's extra clothing hung. There was a small dressing table on the other wall with a looking glass over it.

It was nothing like her room at Uncle William's, not in looks or smells, but still it felt like... home.

Chapter 11

H ANNAH PACED THE LENGTH of the kitchen and back.

Hannah Jr. had the little boys in her care. Tamson and Verity were up in Tamson's room. Joseph was helping Caleb Jr. feed the livestock, but they would be back in time for dinner.

Hannah wanted things resolved beforehand. "I could not turn them away."

"I understand, truly I do, but the village elders—"

"Must answer to God for what they allowed these children to endure." Hannah whirled and faced Caleb, who was seated at the table.

"I do not disagree with thee. Just know that this will cause a disruption in the village and in our home. Not the children—they are welcome to stay. But the reaction from the elders."

"Can they force us from our home?"

"Nay."

"Can they arrest us for anything?"

"I do not believe they have grounds to do so. Since the children came to us. We did not take them away." The twitch of his lips said he knew how close she'd been to doing just that.

"But they can forcibly remove the children, can they not?"

"I fear that is the truth of it."

"Can we do nothing to prevent them?"

He spread his hands, palms up. "What would thee have me to do? Greet them at the door with my musket?"

The very thought of her gentle husband wielding a weapon toward another human being was shocking—and more than a little alarming, because she almost wished he would. Another thought to repent of later. She was growing quite a list of them.

"First, we must send word to Widow Scudder that they are here and safe. She may not be a good guardian"—he ignored her unladylike snort—"but she will be worried. The girl was missing the entire night."

Hannah lowered her chin, palm to her forehead. "Thee are right, of course. Will thee send Caleb Jr. after supper?"

"I will. And then"—he stood from his chair—"I suspect we had best ready ourselves for our unwelcome guests to follow."

The Puritan village elders.

"We should speak to the children first, of course. Ours as well as Verity and Joseph."

"Aye. After thy fine soup and bread." He drew in a deep breath and blew it out. "It smells wonderful, and I am starving."

Hannah bustled around setting the table, including two extra places, then ladled the soup into bowls and called the children. They all took their seats, Verity beside Tamson and Joseph next to Caleb Jr.

"'Tis our custom to pray in silence, words between thee and the Lord alone," Caleb explained to the newcomers.

"Papa coughs and then we can eat," said Benji.

"I will clear my throat, not cough." Caleb glanced sideways at their five-year-old, who squirmed and bowed his head.

After the prayer, Hannah passed around a plate of sliced bread. Verity took one slice, but Joseph helped himself to three after Caleb Jr. did the same. She'd need to bake again, but it was more than worth it to fill their bellies.

Caleb finished his soup and pushed the bowl toward the middle of the table. He turned to Verity first. "Would thee like to stay with us, Verity? To live here with our family?"

The little girl looked first at Joseph, then at Tamson, who nodded encouragement, before sending a shy glance toward Caleb. "I would."

"And thee, Joseph? Would thee like to stay with us?" he asked.

The boy shook his head. "In a few months, I will be twelve and old enough to apprentice."

"And do thee have someone in mind to apprentice with?" Caleb asked.

"Aye. The brewer. His son suggested it, but I have not yet approached him."

"I see." Caleb rubbed his chin. "Thomas, the brewer, has our son Robert apprenticed to him already."

Joseph's expression fell.

"But I have heard that he is selling his ale and cider in Salem Town and a couple of other towns, as well as here in the village. I suspect he could use more help. If thee wish, I would speak to the village elders on thy behalf and see if they would allow thee to start that apprenticeship a little early, under the circumstances."

"You would do that for me? Honest?" The way he spoke that last word made Hannah's heart hurt again. How many people had promised the boy things in the past that had never happened?

"I suspect the elders will be here after supper this evening. I am sending Caleb Jr. to the widow's cottage—"

Verity gasped, her face blanched.

"Fear not." Hannah reached across in front of Tamson and gripped the girl's hand. "Caleb will speak to the elders on thy behalf."

"Will they... will they take me away?" The poor girl's voice was thick with unshed tears.

"Not if I can help it." Hannah shot Caleb a look, and his answering glance said he, too, saw the naked fear in the girl's face. They couldn't send her back. They just... couldn't.

As Hannah dried the last bowl, the jingle of harnesses reached the kitchen. Rags barked in greeting, and Hannah Jr. froze while wiping the table.

"They wasted no time." Hannah stacked the bowl with the rest on the shelf, then folded the damp towel and hung it over its bar next to the stove to dry. "'Tis best to get it over and done with."

"Do thee think they will remove Joseph and Verity tonight?" Hannah Jr. asked.

"I know not. But if the Lord wills, the children will remain here." Hannah removed her apron and smoothed the front of her dress. Caleb would have heard them as well and be on his way in from his carpentry shop in the barn. She needed his steady strength and support to face those men who all looked down on them.

Not all. That wasn't fair. The Buffingtons had always been polite and obliging. But unless Thomas was one of the elders approaching, that man's kindness did them little good this evening.

"Take the children upstairs and keep them quiet," she said to her daughter. Not that Verity would need to be hushed. The girl barely spoke at all, and when she did, it was almost in a whisper.

Hannah Jr. left the kitchen as Caleb entered through the back door.

"Are thee ready to face the lions in the den?" His words were light, but the crease on his forehead and the tightness around his mouth revealed his worries.

"At least 'tis our den, and not theirs." Would that make a difference?

Caleb shucked out of his muffler and overcoat, and then hung his hat on its peg by the back door. He was still a fine figure of a man, for all his forty-two years. And even though they were pacifists, this evening he carried himself like a man ready to do battle.

For the children, but mostly for her. She'd never loved him any more than she did at that moment. Something of her emotions must have reached him.

"There now." He pulled her into his arms. "We have been through worse than this in the past."

That was true, but it had been long ago, and she didn't like to dwell on those years. She laid her head against his shoulder. "'Twas when Hannah Jr. was just a babe in arms. 'Tis all the harder when the innocent are involved."

"Aye. Thee are right." His chest moved beneath her cheek with his sigh. "'Tis the innocent who suffer much for the pride and arrogance of their elders."

"We have to stop it, at least this once, here in our home."

When boot heels thumped on their front porch, he released her and moved into the hall. He opened the door before they knocked. "Gentlemen." He stepped to the side and ushered them in. "Thee are welcome in our home."

Several of the Puritan men glanced at each other as if... as if what? As if they were walking into a trap by being invited into their home? Hannah had to squelch the anger that stirred in her middle lest it show on her face. Anger would do them no good this evening.

The first man, with a long face and narrow nose, entered, and the other two followed. The last was Thomas Buffington, but his solemn face didn't raise Hannah's hopes.

"Are you Caleb Buffum?" The first man asked, ignoring Hannah altogether.

"I am. Will thee not join us in the parlor? We can make introductions in a more comfortable setting." Caleb led the way, not waiting for them to answer.

Hannah followed them in, even though the first man who had entered frowned at her. She'd heard that Puritan women were far more restricted than women among the Friends, but if he thought to shut her out of her own parlor, he was sorely mistaken. She perched on the edge of the settee, and Caleb joined her once the other men had taken seats in the ladderback chairs around the room.

Puffing himself up like a partridge, the first man said, "I am the pastor at Salem Village, Samuel Parris." He pointed to the man next to him. "This is Nathaniel Ingersoll, proprietor of the tavern. And I am given to understand that you already know Thomas Buffington."

"Indeed, we do," Caleb said. "Our Robert is apprenticed to Thomas." He put his hand on Hannah's arm. "This is my goodwife, Hannah."

"I assume you know why we are here." The pastor managed to look down his long nose at them even while seated.

"'Tis about the orphan children, Verity and Joseph." Hannah kept her voice even but firm.

"How did they come to be here, in your home?" He kept his eyes on Caleb, apparently determined to ignore her.

"I had met Verity yesterday while walking along the road." Hannah spoke before Caleb could, determined not to be relegated to the status of a rug. "The girl was hungry. I gave her bread and cheese. She was also in great pain, so I offered her shoes that would fit her."

"And she came away with you?" Thomas asked.

"Not at that time. When she understood that we were Friends—whom thee call Quakers—she became frightened and ran away, even though her feet hurt her terribly." Hannah spread her hands, palms up. "Thee might wish a physician to attend to her feet, but I believe they will heal with decent footwear and rest."

"The children arrived here at our farm around noon today," Caleb picked up the story. "'Tis my understanding that young Joseph led the girl here after she spent the night in a cave, just her and her dog."

"The orphan girl has a dog?" The pastor's expression hovered between aghast and annoyed.

"I believe the dog is the reason she did not return to Widow Scudder's cottage." Hannah glanced at Thomas. His daughter was not much older than Verity, and he didn't look down on the Friends. Of the three of them, he should be the most sympathetic toward the girl. "She feared the old woman would have the animal killed. 'Twould seem she only came upon the dog yesterday before we met on the road, after someone kicked it into the alley."

"The village is not paying Widow Scudder to feed a dog." The pastor crossed his arms. "She *should* eliminate the beast rather than take food from the mouths of the children for its upkeep."

Hannah opened her mouth, but Caleb touched her arm again.

"The children were already hungry before she found the dog," Caleb said. "Both are painfully thin and were filthy when they arrived, wearing clothing not adequate to the season. My goodwife has bathed, fed, and clothed them." He pulled in a long breath before adding. "'Twould appear that the good widow is no longer capable of doing so."

"Widow Scudder has taken in orphans for years," the pastor said. "She knows what she is about."

She was about using those orphans as slave labor to support her, but Hannah didn't say it out loud. "Things become more difficult to manage in one's old age. Perhaps the widow is simply unable to attend to the needs of children anymore."

"We are none of us as young as we used to be." Thomas's tone brought some levity into the room.

"We should like to examine the children for ourselves." The pastor's tone had no levity at all, and Hannah suspected it never did. With his nose held so high, he looked like someone breathing in a bad odor.

Or maybe it was just his disapproval of Caleb and her.

"Before I bring them into the parlor"—Hannah rose and picked up the laundry basket with the children's dirty rag clothing—"this is what they were wearing when they arrived today." She thrust the basket under the pastor's nose. If he insisted on looking as if he smelled something unpleasant, then she'd provide what he needed. She lifted out Verity's shoes, the leather ends stained with blood that had seeped from around her nails, and showed them to the gentlemen. "Thee can see the condition they arrived in was very poor, indeed. Their bodies were no cleaner than these rags."

Thomas looked stricken.

With a grimace, the tavern keeper turned his face to the side.

The pastor waved the offending basket away. "Bring the orphans in now."

His voice carried a note of authority that Hannah wanted to balk at, but it wouldn't do to antagonize the man. Odious or not, he carried a great deal of authority in the village. She went into the hall and called up the stairs. "Hannah Jr., please bring Joseph and Verity down to the parlor."

The footfalls were immediate, so the children had been listening. Had the gentlemen listened too? Really listened, with their hearts as well as their ears?

Chapter 12

VERITY TWISTED HER FINGERS deep into the clean fabric of the blue dress Tamson had given her. She didn't want to go downstairs. She didn't want the elders to take her back to the widow's shack. Hannah Jr. took her hand, and Verity clung to it. "Must I?"

"Joseph is already halfway down the steps. Come now." Hannah Jr.'s voice was coaxing, her grip reassuring. "Be as brave as he is."

"I am not so brave. I am scared."

Tamson came to Verity's other side. "I shall stay here and pray until thee have the right answer."

Hannah Jr. shot her sister a glance that Verity couldn't interpret, then focused on her again. "I wish I could say that they will allow thee to stay, but we cannot know until we go down. Are thee ready now?"

She'd never be ready. Part of her wanted to run away, and another part wanted to throw up her dinner. With a whine, Button pushed his nose into the hand she still had tangled in her dress. She let go of the fabric and stroked his soft fur.

"Button will stay up here with Tamson," Hannah Jr. said.

"I will keep him out of their sight." Tamson knelt and wrapped her arms around the half-grown pup.

Hannah Jr. gave a slight tug on Verity's hand, just enough to get her feet moving. Every step rang hollow beneath the heels of her new shoes, and then they were downstairs at the door where the Puritan men sat beyond. One looked scary, and another looked tired. The third had a jolly appearance, his waistcoat filled with an ample belly. His round spectacles framed kind eyes with creases in the corners.

Uncle William had worn similar spectacles, and he'd called his eye creases smile lines. If only Uncle William were still here.

Hannah Jr. led Verity into the room and remained standing beside her, keeping a steady hold on her hand, the other arm across her shoulders.

"Children." Hannah sat next to Caleb. "These are the village pastor, the tavern keeper, and the brewer."

"Brewer?" Joseph perked up. He'd moved to stand at Hannah Jr.'s other side. "Benjamin's father?"

"Aye, that would be me," the jolly man said. "'Twas he who helped you cut firewood."

The pastor shot the other man a look of displeasure.

Verity shrank back against Hannah Jr.

Joseph gave the brewer a nod. "I very much enjoyed working beside him."

"And he spoke highly of you, young man."

"Aye, well"—the pastor gestured to the tavern keeper—"as we have no physician until Dr. Griggs arrives, please bring the children closer so that Nathaniel may examine them. He has some experience with matters of health."

If Verity could have burrowed underneath Hannah Jr.'s skirts, she would have, but the gentle young lady led her and Joseph to the tired-looking man. Up close, he looked even more tired, but not mean. He held out his hand to Joseph first, who stepped forward bravely.

The man poked and prodded, listened to Joseph's chest, and looked down his throat. Then he faced the pastor. "The boy appears in good health, but not good condition. I can plainly feel his ribs as well as the bones in his back."

That didn't seem to make the pastor happy. His forehead creased and deepened his frown.

"What he needs is good food and plenty of it," the man continued, unmindful of the pastor's reaction. "It attests to the Quakers' account of the widow not adequately feeding the boy."

Nathaniel shooed Joseph back to Hannah Jr.'s side and extended a hand to Verity.

She couldn't move. What if he said the widow had fed her enough? What if he sent her back to the filthy shack? What if the widow killed Button?

"Come, girl. I will not hurt you." The tavern keeper's voice was low and kind. When Hannah Jr. transferred her hand to his, his touch was gentle on her fingers.

She wanted to snatch it back, but where could she go? They would fetch her back from Tamson's room. The cave was too cold. That only left the shack. Her knees trembled.

"What fears you so, child?"

"The widow." The words came before she could stop them. Not that she wanted to stop them, exactly, but she didn't want to talk to the man either.

Genuine concern creased his brow. "Has she hurt you?"

Verity shook her head.

"Then why do you fear her?"

"She would kill Button." He seemed to wait for her to continue, so she summoned her strength to speak up. "She will not let me eat if I do not collect enough rags. I have to sleep on a hard wooden shelf. The floor of the shack is dirt, and there is no place to bathe or wash my clothing." A slight sob escaped her. "She took away my clean dresses and sold them, along with Momma's shawl pin." Another sob stopped her words.

"Oh, child." The jolly man leaned forward.

The reverend raised a hand toward him. "The widow is within her rights. She would have sold it to purchase food. A commendable decision."

Verity wasn't exactly sure what *commendable* meant. She just wanted Momma's shawl pin back.

"Would thee examine her feet?" Hannah asked from behind, stopping Verity's words. "I saw no infection, but I would rest easier if thee would confirm it."

"Sit on my knee, child."

Verity allowed the tavern owner to lift her. Hannah Jr. steadied her while he removed her shoes and stockings. He ran his fingers over her toes, spreading and looking between them and bending her knees to see the bottoms of her feet.

He glanced at Hannah across the room. "You provided her with these shoes?"

"I did."

He grunted and helped Verity off his knee. "Bless you for that." The reverend shot him a sour look, but he paid the man no mind. "The girl is also underfed, and if Mrs. Buffum had not intervened, could have been crippled in another fortnight, or frostbitten from going barefoot in the snow. 'Tis clear, in my opinion, that Widow Scudder is no longer capable of caring for these orphans."

"Are you saying we must find another home for them?" The pastor's voice was too loud.

Verity ducked behind Hannah Jr., holding her shoes and stockings to her middle.

"My son mentioned that young Joseph would like to be apprenticed to me," the jolly man said, and Joseph grinned at him in return. "This is agreeable to me. I am told he is not quite twelve years old, as is our custom, but I believe,"—he cleared his throat—"that under the circumstances, we can hasten his apprenticeship."

"Thank you, sir," Joseph said, then added, "Becky is still with the widow. She is thirteen."

Verity peeked from behind Hannah Jr.

"There is another one?" The pastor glared around the room.

"Goodie Biddle could use the help of a girl that age," the tavern keeper said. "She has three children, the oldest just five, and another on the way. Her husband provides well for them. I can assure you that she will feed and see to the girl's care."

"A good Puritan family." The pastor seemed somewhat pleased with that. Then he glared at Verity. "But what is to be done with this one?"

"She is welcome to stay with us." Caleb's words deepened the pastor's frown. "We can provide for her, with food, clothing, *and* the love of a family."

The love of a family. Verity wanted to run to him and throw her arms around him, but she couldn't move. The pastor's stare held her in place like a frightened mouse under the watchful eyes of a cat.

"She is a Puritan girl," he said at last. "'Twould be most egregious to leave her in the hands of a—"

"Of a man and his family who believe in the God of the universe?" There was an edge to Caleb's voice that hadn't been there before, and Verity turned her head to look at him. "The One who created and loves us all?" He stood and looked down at the gathered guests. "The One who charged us to care for the widow and the orphan?"

Hannah rose beside him.

They stood in Verity's defense.

Hope fluttered in her chest. She let go of Hannah Jr.'s hand, dropped her shoes, and raced barefoot toward them.

Hannah stooped and opened her arms.

Verity flung herself into them, clinging with all her might.

Hannah straightened, lifting Verity with her, and faced the Puritan men again.

The men had also risen from their seats.

Joseph and Hannah Jr. had backed to the side of the room, out of the way of the silent war that raged across the space.

Then the jolly man cleared his throat. "'Tis obvious that Mr. Buffum more than adequately provides for his family. The girl would prosper here on such a well-kept farm. Further, 'tis apparent that she chooses to stay."

"She is but a child and knows not what is good for her," the reverend snapped. "She needs the church and its teaching and—"

"The widow never brought her orphans to church," the tavern-keeper said. "'Twas a bone of contention from the beginning, what with her being paid a monthly stipend to provide for them."

"'Tis true." The jolly man pinned the reverend with a sharp look from behind his round spectacles. "We have all known she failed to provide for them in that manner. And yet, we did not intervene."

The pastor pointed a finger at Verity. "Would you leave her to spiritual decay in the home of a Quaker?" He practically shouted at the other two Puritans.

"We left her to physical *and* spiritual decay with the widow, did we not?" The tavern-keeper's words were softly spoken, in contrast to the irate pastor.

The jolly man removed his spectacles and wiped them with a handkerchief. Facing the reverend, he slid them back onto his face. "Are you willing to take the child into your home and keep her under your care?"

Verity gasped, and Hannah hugged her tighter. She didn't want to go with the pastor, even if he did have a daughter her age. She wanted to stay here and sleep in Tamson's room on a real bed with sheets and a pillow, Button on a rug on the floor beside her.

After a brittle pause, the pastor said, "You know my situation. I have barely enough to provide for my household now, and am still awaiting the firewood that was promised to me." He shot a sour look at the jolly man.

"With winter at our doorstep, I know not who else would have provisions set aside to add to their household now," the jolly man said. "I can make room for Joseph, but not for the girl."

He didn't look at Verity, but he seemed in favor of her staying with the Buffums. For that, she liked him very much. It eased her mind that Joseph would be going with this kind man, and not the reverend.

"Neither can I take the girl, I am sorry to say." The tavern-keeper raised his hands and let them drop. "My wife's sister and her family arrive tomorrow to stay the winter with us. They lost everything in a house fire in Andover last week. 'Twill strain my provisions as far as I am able to care for them."

Another lengthy silence stretched across the room as the tavern-keeper and the jolly man faced the pastor. None of them resumed their seats.

Verity trembled, and Hannah swayed with her, rocking her and humming in a low tone as Momma had done so long ago. Verity breathed in deeply, the scent of Hannah's hair filling her. Hannah didn't smell like Momma, but the swaying, the arms around her, and the humming all combined to overwhelm Verity. She broke into sobs.

"Let us leave things as they are, shall we?" Hannah said. "Verity has been through enough for today. The child needs to be put to bed."

The woman turned her back on the Puritans and ushered Verity into the hall and up the stairs.

Hannah and Tamson helped her strip down to her new shift, then tucked her into Tamson's bed. Sitting beside her, Hannah stroked her hair. "Thee will be all right."

"I wi-wish to st-stay with you," Verity sobbed, her whole body shaking.

"I know thee do." Dampness gathered in Hannah's eyes. "I wish it as well. Shall we pray together and ask God to help us?"

"In silence?" Verity wanted to hear Hannah's words because she couldn't think of any of her own. Maybe she had been away from church for too long. Maybe she was already a heathen, too sinful to know how to pray anymore. Fear gripped her.

"Be easy." Hannah's voice was as soothing as her hands. "I shall pray out loud if thee prefer."

Relief rushed over her. "Please." She folded her hands and squeezed her eyes shut.

"Our Father God, through the Light of Christ Jesus, please turn the heart of the one downstairs who would prevent this dear child from staying with us. Convict him that she is where Thee would have her to be. Allow us to bring Verity into our family forever. Amen."

Forever. Verity opened her eyes. "Will God do it?"

"If He wills, aye."

"When will we know?"

Hannah shook her head. "God's timing is not our timing. But for now, thee are safe here, warm and fed."

Button whined from the side of the bed.

"Thee as well, Button, are welcome here." Hannah petted the red-and-white head, its chin resting on the edge of the covers, but she looked at Verity. "And if thee must leave us, know this. If Button cannot go with thee, he is safe with us. He would have a home here."

"Even if I must go back to the widow?"

"Thee will *not* be returned to the widow, that much I can promise thee," Hannah said with conviction.

That reassurance, the guarantee of Button's safety, and all the drama of the day settled over Verity. As much as she wanted to enjoy Hannah's time and attention, her eyelids grew too heavy to lift.

Chapter 13

V ERITY ROUSED TO SUNLIGHT on her face. She snuggled deeper under the soft quilt. Then her eyes popped open, and she sat bolt upright.

It hadn't been a dream.

She was in Tamson's room. The light streamed in from a window framed with a curtain. The space on the bed beside her was empty, but Verity had a vague remembrance of Tamson sleeping there. She looked over the edge to the raggedy blanket Hannah had given her, folded into a square, and Button asleep on top of it.

The pup raised his head, stood, and shook himself. He stretched, yawned, his pink tongue ending in a perfect curl.

"'Tis true, Button." She rubbed his head. "We are still here."

A gentle tap sounded on the door right before it opened. Tamson came in, carrying a wooden tray with a bowl and cup on it. "Good morning, sleepyhead. Mother said to let thee sleep thyself out this morning, but thee must be starving by now. 'Tis nearly eight o'clock."

As if on cue, Verity's stomach rumbled.

Tamson set the tray on her lap and settled next to her. "Did thee sleep well?"

"Aye." The scent of cinnamon rose with the steam from a bowl of thick porridge. So thick that Verity needed the horn spoon to eat it. She took a mouthful. It was sweet with molasses, and so different from the type of watery gruel she'd eaten for weeks, that she swallowed it almost without chewing and shoved in another bite.

"Not too fast," Tamson said. "No one will take it away from thee. Mother makes the best oatmeal there is. 'Twould be almost sinful to not enjoy it."

Sinful? Verity set the spoon down. That was the last thing she wanted to be. Sin would send her straight to the fiery place where bad people went. She shivered.

"Are thee cold?"

"Nay." She pushed the bowl to the other side of the tray, but Tamson pushed it back.

"Mother says thee must eat every bite, and I am to stay here until thee do."

"I do not wish to sin."

Tamson cocked her head as if confused. "Why would thee sin?"

"You said if I did not enjoy the porridge, 'twould be sinful."

The other girl clapped a hand over her mouth, then dropped it. "Hannah Jr. is always telling me to mind my words. 'Twas only a jest, I promise. There is nothing sinful about eating oatmeal."

"Are you sure?" Because Verity desperately wanted to clean the bowl of its goodness.

"Upon my word. Please, eat thy breakfast or Mother will be very upset with me."

Keeping her eyes on Tamson, Verity reached for the spoon. At the other girl's encouraging nod, she took another bite. The sweet warmth filled her mouth and heated her insides all the way down, but she didn't gulp it again. Still, the bowl was empty in no time. Then she picked up the cup and took a sip of the warm milk. Had anything ever tasted so good?

"Now we can get thee dressed and start our day." Tamson hopped off the bed. "I pulled another of my old dresses from the trunk in the attic." She raised the gray fabric to her face and sniffed, wrinkling her nose. "'Twill need a proper washing later, but 'tis good enough to do chores. I am to show thee around the farm, and thee are to learn what chores are our responsibility."

"Our responsibility?" Verity allowed herself to be pulled from the bed and stood still while Tamson lowered the musty-smelling dress over her shift.

"Aye. Thee cannot be a part of this family without having assigned chores." Tamson giggled. "Unless thee are Jonathan, of course. He is but three years old."

Tamson kept chattering as she combed and braided Verity's hair, but Verity heard little of it.

A part of this family.

The words kept circling in Verity's head.

She'd loved Uncle William and missed him with a deep ache, but to be part of a family again, with other children... that was like a dream come true. Dare she believe it could happen? Dare she be happy for it?

Or would the sour-faced reverend from the Puritan church come and haul her back to Widow Scudder's?

Hannah rested her hands on the windowsill in the parlor where she'd been dusting. Tamson and Verity ran through the inch of snow that had fallen overnight, girlish squeals of delight drifting through the crisp air. Tamson did the squealing, but Verity was running beside her with barely a limp, holding onto the older girl's hand while Button raced in circles around them.

Poor Verity needed a mother—needed a family. Hannah was prepared to make a stand to bring her permanently into theirs. After all, Verity was already here, and of her own choosing. That should count for something.

Caleb would support her, she'd no doubt of that. He'd remind her of all the problems that could arise, but in the end, his heart was as open as hers to bringing Verity into the family. He was like that, her husband, of sound mind and squishy heart. The children would welcome her as well.

Tamson had wished for another girl when Benji was born, and again when Jonathan followed two years after him. Hannah had thought she was done during the barren seven years between Tamson and Benji, but God had been gracious and had given her the little boys. Was He now giving her another daughter?

Oh. She turned from the window and sank onto the closest chair. She pressed her hand to her middle. After all the years and five other children born, she still missed the one they'd lost. A daughter.

A *clang* rose from the kitchen. Hannah Jr.'s voice followed as she gently scolded one of the boys. Outside, a rooster crowed, too late for his sunrise duty. A log shifted in the fireplace, sending a shower of sparks up the chimney in a fragrant rush. Normal things happening all around her.

But God might be giving her—Hannah Buffum—another daughter.

Tears simmered on her bottom lids. Who was she to wage a battle against the elders of the village? Shame pushed a single tear over the edge. Who was she to say where Verity belonged or didn't belong? Was not God alone the father of orphans? Did He not love the girl more than Hannah could ever hope to? Was He not more concerned for Verity's welfare than she could ever be?

Then why had He left her in the widow's care?

Hannah flinched at the thought. *I am sorry, Lord, for doubting Thee. I cannot understand Thy ways, but I know them to be true, to be good, and to be just. Help me through my doubts.*

"Hannah?" Caleb's voice entered the parlor a moment before he did. "There thee are. I wondered if thee would—" He stopped short, then crossed the room and knelt beside her chair, dark brows drawn together. "What has happened?"

"Nothing." Her voice came out steady, but inside she wanted to sob.

Her claim of nothing wasn't true, and they both knew it. He opened his mouth, then snapped it shut and waited. He'd probably wait like that all day if need be, giving her time to find her words.

"I was doubting God's wisdom in allowing Verity to be with Widow Scudder." Hannah twisted the dust rag between her hands. "I so want to fight to keep her, but if 'tis God's will that she be with us, He will gift her to us."

Caleb sat back on his heels. "Exactly so."

"'Tis just that I want..." She turned her face away, trying to squash her own desires.

"God knows what thee want, my love." With a gentle finger on her chin, Caleb turned her face back to him. "And He delights in giving good gifts to His children. The Bible says that."

"Aye. But what if He does not think she should..." She couldn't finish the sentence.

"Then He has something better in mind for her."

It hurt to think that anything could be better than their family, than the love already growing in Hannah's heart for little Verity, which had bloomed almost from the first moment she'd seen her. And Tamson's joy at having another sister, what about that?

None of it mattered unless it was within God's will.

She leaned against Caleb's shoulder. "Thee have a selfish and willful wife, I fear."

"If thee were perfect, thee would be too fine for a simple man like me." There was a chuckle in his voice. "But thee are the most caring woman I know, and for that, I am very thankful to the Lord for bringing us together all those years ago." He backed up and looked her in the eyes. "After all, 'twould have been most inconvenient to have the children without thee."

The laugh that he brought her threatened to be part sob, but it felt good. It released some of her pain. She could always count on Caleb to see the bright side of anything, even when she didn't really want him to.

He sobered. "I believe, in my heart, that God has brought this child to us for a purpose. Will she stay forever? I cannot tell thee. She is here now, so let us enjoy whatever time God allows us to have with her, shall we?"

Was that the best they could do?

She'd done it again, longed to do something that was beyond her power. Tried to wrest control of the situation away from God.

Forgive me, Lord, and continue to forgive me as I struggle to accept Your will—not mine—for this child.

The red hen's beady eyes fixed on Verity as she stood next to the nesting box. "Are you sure she will not bite me?"

"Chickens are not biters. They have no teeth," Tamson said. "They peck, and it hurts a little, but not like a bite."

"I think I would rather not be pecked, either." Verity kept her hands behind her back.

"Let me show thee." Tamson crooned to the hen while she slipped her hand underneath the fluffy bird and withdrew two dark brown eggs. "'Tis all there is this morning. The hens are coming into their winter break."

"What is their winter break?" Verity settled the eggs Tamson handed her into a basket they'd brought from the kitchen.

"When the days get shorter, the hens will lay fewer eggs. Have thee never had chickens?"

"I cannot remember them in Maine, and Uncle William did not keep any in Salem Town."

"Thee lived in Maine?" Tamson scooped three more eggs from under another bird and handed them to Verity.

"With Momma and Papa, and my brother and sister too."

"What happened?" Tamson asked the question as one might inquire of the weather, but it struck Verity like a stone.

"My brother died of a fever, and then months later, Indians came and killed everyone else."

With a gasp, Tamson whirled around. "Indians? However did thee escape?"

"Momma had sent me to the fort to buy salt. When I got back, everyone was dead."

There'd been blood everywhere. Why hadn't she remembered that until now? Papa slumped over against their wagon with arrows in his chest. Momma on the ground outside the cabin door, the grass around her blond hair red and sticky, Verity's baby sister in her arms, sightless eyes open to the sky.

Verity dropped the basket of eggs with a sickening crack, and then the whole story tumbled out of her. She'd never even told Uncle William all those details, or how she'd raced the half mile to their closest neighbor for help, only to find them dead as well. It had taken her hours to reach the fort again, and she couldn't remember a step of the journey. She'd not spoken to anyone. Not a word. Not until Uncle William came for her many days later.

Tamson's arms were around her, holding her close, tears streaking her face as she listened.

"And then I did everything I could think of to save Uncle William, but he died too." Verity finished her story, voice hoarse and lashes so tear-laden she could barely see.

"Thee are such a brave girl." Tamson pushed her back far enough to look her in the eye. "A very brave and very special girl. I am sorry thee had to go through all of that, and then the widow, too. I am very glad thee are here now. Very glad thee were brave enough to come yesterday."

"I broke the eggs." Would Hannah think her less special when she learned of that? Or would she turn Verity away? After all, wasting food was a sin. The widow had said so. "Hannah will not be pleased."

"Who cares about the eggs? Mother will understand." Tamson gave Verity's shoulders a little shake. "'Tis nothing to worry thyself over. But Verity?"

"Aye?"

"Thank thee for sharing thy story with me. Nothing that happened was thy fault. Not what happened to thy parents nor the sickness that took away thy uncle."

"But maybe if I had not sinned in some way they—"

"Nay. 'Twas not anything thee did. 'Twas Indians and illness, things far beyond our ability to control. My parents are often chiding me for trying to control too much when 'tis God's place, not mine."

That didn't make sense. "Why would God want Momma and Papa dead? Or Uncle William? God is good—not bad."

"God is good. But sometimes He allows bad things to happen, and we cannot understand why. 'Tis just"—Tamson shrugged—"the way life is."

Uncle William had said much the same thing when Verity had first gone to live with him. He'd reassured her that none of it had been her fault, but deep down, she hadn't believed him. And yet, searching the sincere gray eyes of her new friend, she found not a shadow of doubt. Could it be? Was she not to blame?

"Would it be all right if I shared your story with my parents? It might help them understand thee better. Unless thee would rather tell them thyself?"

"I do not think I can speak of it again. Maybe not ever."

"Then I shall. But only to them, no one else. I promise."

They remained in the chicken coop for a long time, holding each other, while the chickens squawked around them. In the dusty sunbeam from the coop's high windows, Verity felt cleansed.

Chapter 14

"**A**RE THEE SURE?" HANNAH straightened her bonnet while seated at her dressing table, watching Caleb in the looking glass.

"We cannot hide away with Verity and pray that nothing happens."

"I know." She dropped her hands to her lap. "But driving through the village and to attend meeting might seem as if we are taunting the village elders." Although they had little choice, as the meetinghouse was on the opposite side of the village from their farm. Unless Caleb took the wagon off the road, which would be a very bumpy and uncomfortable ride for all of them, through the village was the only way to get there.

"We must not forsake the fellowship that we have among ourselves because of the opinions—or actions—of man." Caleb's voice was firm, as was the strong line of his jaw.

They would attend meeting and that was that.

After five days of ups and downs—with Verity coming to them, the village elders following, Hannah's revelation that she was not in control, Verity telling her story to Tamson, who shared it with her and Caleb, and shuffling around to fit another member into their household, not to mention the worry that the elders would descend on them again and whisk Verity away...

Hannah's nerves were stretched well beyond her comfort.

"Unfortunately, I did not have time to remove the wagon's cover this week with all the goings-on." Despite her husband's stern face, his brown eyes gleamed at her in the looking glass.

Hannah turned around on the dressing table's bench. "Thank thee for that."

"We may have need of it before we return. Caleb Jr. says the air smells of snow, and he is often correct in these things." Indeed, their oldest son had shown a knack for predicting the weather from a young age. "'Tis early in the season for a deep snow, but he was concerned enough to keep the cows in the front pasture this morning."

Rising from the bench, Hannah gave Caleb a quick hug. "Hitch the horses. I shall have the children ready in moments." Then she slipped out into the upstairs hall.

Giggles came from around Tamson's door. Nay, that wasn't right. Tamson's and Verity's door.

Hannah Jr. still slept in the nursery with the little boys, as she had done since Benji's birth. That young lady needed to be a mother of her own, but that thought brought back the issue of the Puritan, Benjamin Buffington. Hannah had no energy to tackle another problem.

"Come, children. Father will have the horses hitched soon."

"Already downstairs, Mother," Hannah Jr. called.

Caleb Jr. came out of his bedroom, shrugging into his coat. "I will help him." He pounded down the stairs ahead of her. Could the boy never just walk normally?

Tamson, wearing an impish grin, stuck her head out around her door. "We will be down shortly."

What was she up to? "Be sure thee are."

Hannah went down to the kitchen, already scrubbed clean after their breakfast, and took her heavy shawl from its peg by the back door.

"Mother?" Hannah Jr. approached, keeping her voice low. "Do thee not worry that the village elders may be waiting for us?"

"I have thought of little else all night." The dark circles under Hannah's eyes in the looking glass had borne witness. "But there is nothing we can do. If the Lord wills for Verity to remain with us, He will see it through."

"I know, and the words come easily to my mind and lips, but not so easily to my heart." Hannah Jr. glanced back at the boys, who were stacking wooden blocks on the floor beside the table. "Benji and Jonathan are growing so attached to Verity. I worry for her, of course, but I worry for them as well."

As if the urge to protect Verity weren't enough, the added urge to protect her children from disappointment rose in Hannah. She drew in a deep breath and closed her eyes. *Lord, must we go through this? All of us?* Then she opened her eyes to see Hannah Jr.'s concerned expression. "I choose to trust in the Lord, but I will tell thee this, I must make that choice every day, and sometimes several times throughout the day. 'Tis not easy."

"Nay, 'tis not. I will strive to do better."

"That is all He asks of us."

Why was it so difficult?

"Here we are." Tamson stood in the doorway, shielding Verity from view. When she had their attention, Tamson stepped aside and ushered the other girl into the kitchen, looking every inch a child of the Friends. Tamson had dressed her in a dove gray dress with a fichu tucked in the neckline, a white shawl around her shoulders, and a slightly dented but clean white bonnet with a deep brim shading much of her face.

No one from the village would ever see the little ragpicker in the child who stood before them.

"Verity, thee look ready for meeting." Hannah Jr.'s voice held all the approval in Hannah's heart.

"Come, everyone." Hannah beckoned to the boys. "Father will have the horses ready. Let us go and not be late."

Her step was lighter as they left the house and made their way to the wagon. Between the wagon's covering and Verity's appearance, the gloomy skies overhead wouldn't dampen her hopes that they would pass unnoticed through the village to the meetinghouse and back again.

Tamson had prepared Verity for what the service would be like, explaining that it would be different than what she'd been used to. To start with, they didn't call it *church*, they called it *meeting*. The building wasn't even called a church, it was called a meetinghouse. Inside, it was a large rectangle with two long lines of benches. There was no pulpit at the front, no table draped in linens, and no cross on the wall.

Nobody stood at the front of the building and gave a sermon. Instead of one man speaking at length, several men—and even more surprising, several women—rose and spoke. They didn't even speak on the same subject. Each rose and spoke whatever the Lord had put on his or her heart, according to Tamson, who whispered more explanations as the service went on.

Whispering was strictly prohibited in the Puritan church, perhaps even considered another sin, but Hannah hadn't corrected her daughter or even frowned at her. Neither had anyone else.

Before and after the service, many women and girls came to be introduced to Verity. At first, she wanted to hide behind Hannah Jr. or Tamson, but she ventured forward and spoke with some of them. They were so friendly. Maybe that was why they called themselves Friends instead of Quakers.

How had Verity ever thought these people to be evil? Why did the Puritans think they were?

By the time they were back in the wagon, Verity's middle was rumbling, despite the large breakfast she'd eaten of pancakes, eggs, and bacon. She sat in the bed of the wagon with her back against the side, Tamson beside her with little Jonathan on her lap. Outside, the wind blew large flakes of snow that were just starting to stick to the trees and coat the ground.

Tamson nudged her with her shoulder. "What did thee think of our service?"

"'Tis much different than the Puritan church." Nothing had frightened her or seemed the least bit evil or wrong. Perhaps, if the Puritans would come to the Quaker meeting, they would see what fine people they were.

"Different meaning better?"

"Tamson." Hannah gave her daughter a pointed look. "That is not a question thee should ask."

"Why?"

"Because it implies that there is something wrong with the Puritan way of worship, and we know not enough about that to judge."

"But Verity does, she used to attend there." Tamson turned to her. "Did thee not?"

"Enough." Hannah's voice told her that was the end of that, and the wagon fell into silence, but not uncomfortably so, until they pulled to a stop.

Robert climbed out and spoke over the tailgate. "See thee next week. 'Twas nice to meet thee, Verity."

"Tell Joseph I miss him," Verity said, and he nodded in response.

The family called out their goodbyes, and then the wagon was moving again. Hannah Jr. kept looking out of the opening in the back of the canvas top, perhaps watching her brother walk away. It must be hard to see him leave them and return to the brewer where he was apprenticed. It must be difficult for him too, leaving such a fine family behind.

Verity sure didn't want to leave them. Not ever.

The world was white and still the next morning, windblown snow heaped into sparkling mounds around the farm. Verity enjoyed kicking through it on the way to and from the chicken coop, her feet warm in a pair of boots Tamson had unearthed from a trunk.

"'Tis like something out of a fairytale." Tamson spun, her arms outstretched.

"What is a fairytale?" Verity asked.

Tamson stopped and stared at her. "Thee know not of fairytales?"

Verity shook her head. Fairies were evil, but maybe fairytales meant something different.

"They are stories about people who live in castles, fanciful beasts, elves, fairies, and other magical things."

Fear gripped Verity until her mittened hands trembled on the egg basket's handle, making them rattle inside. Magic was another name for evil. The Puritan preacher had said so in a sermon that had brought her nightmares for weeks afterward. She'd woken crying until Uncle William had held her and reassured her that she was safe.

Had she been wrong about the Quakers? Were they evil after all?

"What is it?" Tamson hurried to her side. "Thee are as white as the snow."

"Magic is evil," Verity blurted out.

Tamson looked confused. "'Tisn't real, thee know. The magic in fairytales is make-believe."

"Make-believe is a lie." Verity hugged the basket to her middle. Lying was one of the worst of sins. What should she do now?

"'Tisn't a lie, 'tis a story." Tamson scratched her head under her knitted wool cap. "Did thy mother never tell thee a story before bed? Something made up to entertain?"

"Not that I remember." Momma had read from the Bible in a soothing tone, the squeak of her rocking chair adding to Verity's sense of comfort and safety.

"Then thee must let me tell thee one."

Verity's fear turned to motion. She threw the basket at Tamson and ran.

Button barked and raced after her, as if he knew something was wrong.

"Verity!" Tamson's shout reached her above the blood pounding in her ears. "Verity, come back!"

That only added speed to her feet. Verity crashed through the brambles she and Joseph had hidden behind just a week before. They scratched at her face and hooked onto her mittens and shawl, but she jerked free and kept running. There was only one place to go.

Joseph's cave.

Hannah pulled on her boots but left her shawl on its peg, taking down Caleb's spare coat instead. She pulled a knitted wool cap over her hair, then faced her distraught daughter.

"I am so sorry," Tamson wailed. "'Tis all my fault."

"Nay. 'Tis not." She pulled Tamson into her arms, looking over her head at Hannah Jr.'s worried frown. "'Tis the way the girl was raised. Thee were not to know."

"'Twas just a story, Mother." Hannah Jr. rested her hand on her sister's shoulder. "Why would it cause Verity such fear?"

"The Puritans believe differently than us. They teach their children to fear sin and evil above all things."

"Thee have taught us that sin and evil are bad, have thee not?"

There wasn't time to get into the nuances. Hannah eased Tamson from her arms to those of her sister. "I will explain at another time. I must find Verity first. Tell thy father what happened and where I have gone. He can follow our prints in the snow, if he decides."

With that, she left the house, finding Verity's footprints and following them beyond the yard and into the forest. What sort of warped teaching had she endured to make her so fearful? Of course sin and evil were bad things, but to fear them beyond common sense was also a bad thing. And a little girl on her own in a forest buried in snow was just plain dangerous.

Fear for Verity warred with anger at those who had driven her to run.

Did the Puritan's never teach of the love of God? His protections, His promises, His provisions for those who loved Him? Was the whole of their lives mired in the darkness of this world instead of accepting the Light of Christ? Were they yet slaves to sin instead of forgiven by the Savior?

The weighty questions plagued her as she ducked under snow-laden branches. The girl wasn't heading for the widow's shack, but she was on a straight course, as if she had a certain destination.

The cave. Of course. Joseph had told them that Verity and Button had slept in a cave the night before he brought her to the farm. She must be headed there. But would she be able to find it in the snow?

Another set of tracks cut across Verity's, or perhaps the girl had cut across those tracks. Hannah stopped and squinted into the murkiness of the forest. Those tracks seemed to follow a deer path, a narrow opening between the trees and brush. Who else would be out on such an unseasonably cold morning?

There had not been a sighting of Indians in their area for a couple of years, but rumors had reached the village of Indians prowling around other nearby settlements. Rumors—not facts—but a tingle of fear shot through her all the same.

Hannah bent and examined the tracks as best she could in the fluffy snow. She pressed her fingers into the outline of a boot's heel. Not moccasins. Not Indians. With relief, she continued to follow Verity's tracks, easy to distinguish with Button's prints beside her.

Until they stopped.

Chapter 15

V ERITY HUDDLED AGAINST THE cold cave wall with Button in her arms, the dog warming her as much as comforting her. The hole above her was ringed in snow, dimming the light it let in. But sounds carried across the frigid air, crisp and clear. The tread of boots, crunching against the snow.

Was it Tamson? Had the girl followed her clear out here? Fear still gripped her heart, but it warred with the cold of her fingers buried in Button's fur and the icy chill of dried tears on her cheeks. She couldn't survive in the cave. She couldn't return to the widow. The village elders had as much as said that nobody else would take her in. That meant returning to Buffums' farm... eventually.

"Verity?" Hannah's voice was soft and close to the concealed opening of the cave.

Button whined and wiggled to get free.

"Hush, be still," she whispered against his fur, tightening her hold on him.

"Where are thee, Verity?" The footsteps had stopped. "Please. Will thee not return with—" Her voice broke off.

Other voices reached Verity, but from the hole above, not from the cave's mouth. She couldn't make out the words, but they carried a cadence, like a chant of some sort. Verity's already cold arms broke out in goosebumps. Could it be the pastor's daughter and niece again with the slave woman?

Joseph had been worried by their behavior. He'd been worried about the Buffums too, but not once he and Verity had arrived at the farm.

Verity had once wanted to meet the girls in the forest, but not now. Not after meeting the preacher. He scared her worse than Tamson's fairytales. Well, just as much, anyway.

"Verity?" Hannah's whisper carried a note of something that made Verity shiver even more.

Button must have heard it too, because he whined and squirmed again, this time slipping from her cold fingers.

Before she could grab him, he ran out of the cave.

The chanting voices grew louder as Verity huddled alone in the darkness.

Chanting in the forest. Hannah clutched the collar of Caleb's coat closer around her throat. Whoever was out there, they were up to no good. She couldn't make out all the words, but those she heard sent a chill into her soul. They were female voices, and she'd clearly seen the heel print, or else she would have thought them Indians for sure. Once, long ago, she'd heard Indians chant around a fire.

An experience she would never forget.

Then Button seemed to materialize out of the rock and race toward Hannah. She stooped and stroked his fur. "Where is she?"

A pink tongue washed her face in response.

Hannah rose and followed the pup's tracks to the rock wall. Once up close, a narrow opening, too narrow for Hannah to fit, allowed Button to race inside.

"Verity, dear. Please come out." She kept her voice to a whisper, not wishing whoever was chanting to overhear and investigate. "There are others in the forest. Please, come with me. Come home."

Home? The word sank to Verity's chest and lodged there. Tamson's room. The warm kitchen with the brick hearth and long table, surrounded by a family who talked while they ate their meals. And laughed.

Momma had laughed often, a merry sound that Verity sometimes heard in her dreams. Uncle William had been a more sober man—Momma's brother, but older than she. More like a grandfather to Verity. He'd been kind and thoughtful, but not merry.

Button dashed to the cave's doorway again, looked back at her and whined. His tail wagged so hard that his whole back end wiggled as if he wanted to go back to the Buffums' farm. But he returned to Verity and stepped into her lap, tongue washing the dried tears from her cheeks. He'd die out here in the cave. The rats and mice and other things he could have caught would be sleeping the winter away in their holes.

Verity couldn't let Button die.

And she very much wanted to go home—but what about the fairytales?

The person she could ask stood just beyond the cave's opening. Verity nudged Button off her lap and stood.

He woofed and raced to the opening again, looking back at her. He wouldn't leave her, so she had to go with him.

"Verity?"

Pulling her shawl tightly around her for courage, she went to the opening and peered out.

Hannah knelt in the snow, one hand extended. "Oh, my dear. Please, come out."

"Are fairytales evil?" The words burst from her and bounced off the cave's walls.

"They are not evil. Fairytales are make-believe stories where good always wins and evil always loses. But sometimes, the good have to go through bad times, hard times, before they win. Fairytales are stories that teach us lessons in life. Many parents tell them to their children for that purpose."

"Evil always loses?" Verity liked that idea. She took a step into the cave's entrance, and then the chanting grew louder. She shrank back.

"I do not like that chanting either." Hannah reached her hand out again. "Come, let us get away from whoever is doing it."

"'Tis the reverend's daughter and niece, I think. Joseph and I saw them here before, with the slave woman. They were not chanting then. I wanted to meet them, but Joseph would not let me. He said they would not welcome us."

"He is a wise young man. Let us leave the forest and go home now."

The chanting stopped abruptly, and Verity stepped from the cave—into Hannah's embrace.

Relief flowed through Hannah like heated water from the kettle. She buried her nose against Verity's hair and closed her eyes. *Thank Thee, Lord.* Then she pushed the girl back far enough to look into her face. "Thee frightened me when thee ran away."

"I ran because I was afraid." Verity's gray-blue eyes were wide and uncertain.

"There may be other things that will frighten thee in the future, but will thee make me a promise?"

Verity nodded.

"If thee are frightened again, will thee run *to* me and not *away* from me? Give me a chance to set things right with thee. Promise me that?" She held her breath as the girl seemed to think it over.

"I will."

Hannah released her breath in a frosty plume. "Thank thee, dear, for trusting me in this." Then Verity's little arms were around Hannah's neck. She rocked the child back and forth for a long time, there in the snow. It was a small step in Verity's journey to accepting Hannah's love.

"Come." Hannah stood, her toes tingling with cold.

Verity grasped her hand, and they started back, Button trotting ahead of them down the trail they'd left. They hadn't gone more than a quarter of a mile when Caleb appeared. As he drew near, relief filled his eyes.

"So this is where thee have gotten thyselves off to." His dark eyes rested first on Hannah, then on Verity. "Thee are well?"

Verity pressed tighter against Hannah's side, but she nodded.

"Thy feet must be half frozen. Would thee like a lift?" He knelt on the snow and waited.

Hannah could almost feel the struggle within Verity, her fearfulness warring with her desire to be loved and cared for. Soon enough, she found the courage to step forward and crawl onto Caleb's back.

Hannah smoothed the girl's skirts to cover her while Caleb hooked his arms to secure her legs. Then they started toward home.

Where she had crossed the other trail, they came upon two girls and a slave woman, just as Verity had said. The girls were older than Verity, closer to Tamson's age. They ignored Hannah, Caleb, and Verity dressed in their Friends clothing, as most Puritans would. But the slave woman watched them, her face scrunched in what might have been suspicion. Or perhaps Verity's fears were rubbing off on Hannah.

Then she remembered the talk at meeting weeks ago, about the reverend's daughter and niece and his slave. How had she forgotten that? The worry over Verity, of course, but still. Perhaps the slave woman suspected they had spied her chanting in the woods like pagans of old—bringing the young girls with her. Nothing good could come of chanting in the woods like the pagans had.

Hannah would tell Caleb about it once the children were abed. No sense in upsetting Verity again, even if this time, it might be a very real threat of evil.

When they arrived at the house, they were greeted by the rest of the family. Each of them in his or her own way fussed over Verity and Button. Even Rags, the older dog, was happy to see the pup again.

This felt as a family should. Surely God in His wisdom would not allow them to be separated again after this.

Hannah hung the dish towel on its bar to dry and gazed out the window at the white world beyond. December had slipped away, and January had blown in with a vengeance. It had snowed so hard last Sunday that they hadn't ventured into town for meeting. Even with runners attached to the wagon's wheels, it had been too much to ask of the horses.

Barking drew her attention to the barn. Button flounced in the snow, his red ears sometimes all she could see above the drifts. Rags ran after him. Tamson and Verity followed, both bundled in layers until they could barely move. But their laughter brought joy to Hannah's heart. It'd been well over a month since the village elders had left Verity in their care, and there had been not a word from them.

Verity had blossomed. Still skittish as a young heifer if faced with something new, she was learning to adapt. Even more important—to Hannah's way of thinking—were her earnest questions about their faith in God and the Light of Christ. The poor dear had been so traumatized by some of the teachings of the Puritan church that it was slow going, but they were making progress. Quietly. The village elders didn't need to know about that.

Even if they learned, even if they came and wrested the child away from their family, if Hannah and her family could instill in Verity the promise of faith for eternal salvation in Christ, she would be much better off than when she'd arrived.

But it would break Hannah's heart. Already it seemed as if the girl had been born to her, and she suspected Caleb felt the same. He wasn't one to speak about such things, as men in general weren't. It didn't take much, however, to interpret the way his face lit up when Verity addressed him at the dinner table, or the way he watched her play with the little boys.

Hannah turned from the window as the two snow-covered girls and dogs burst through. Faces reddened with cold, eyes bright with life, they giggled as they helped each other unwrap from all the layers of clothing.

"Did thee remember the eggs?" Hannah asked.

"Oh." Tamson's face fell, and she shot a look at Verity. They dissolved into more giggles. "In our pockets, Mother." She drew two brown eggs from each coat pocket, and Verity did the same. "With so few laying now, we decided we needed not the basket. Our hands can keep the eggs warmer inside our pockets."

"I suppose that works in this terrible chill." Leave it to Tamson to work that out. The girl was the cleverest one of her brood. Which could be a blessing... or not. Time would tell with that one.

Another set of boots thumped on the porch just before Caleb came through the door. "Someone is coming from the village." One look at his expression, and Hannah's heart sank.

She hurried back to the window. Two people on horseback, hunched over against the wind. One was larger and heavier while the other was... She pressed her hand to her heart.

"'Tis Robert." She'd know that dark green cap anywhere after spending evenings knitting it the past fall.

"Are thee certain?" Caleb joined her at the window, shedding snow off his coat onto her kitchen floor.

But what did that matter? Robert wouldn't be here unless something were dreadfully wrong. Would he? But Thomas wouldn't bring him out in such weather if he were ill or injured.

The horses plodded toward the barn, where Caleb Jr. stood in the barn doorway, no doubt with dry stalls ready for the tired animals.

"Tamson, the water should be hot in the kettle. Make a pot of tea. Verity, can you take the boys upstairs to their room?" Benji and Jonathan looked up from where they played with blocks in front of the hearth. "Go with her, boys."

Verity lifted Jonathan, and Benji followed them without a fuss.

More than the boys, Hannah wanted Verity out of sight before whoever had come with Robert got to the house. Caleb's raised brow said he understood, but he doubted it would do any good. The only logical person who would arrive with Robert would be Thomas Buffington.

A village elder.

Chapter 16

H ANNAH FORCED HERSELF NOT to hover at the window. Should she offer anything beyond tea to their guest? Should she even think of him as a guest? If there was nothing amiss with Robert, then the reason for the visit was most likely Verity. Tears threatened to clog her throat and stung the backs of her eyes.

Caleb's arms came around her from behind. "We know not why he has come." His breath warmed her ear.

"Who is it?" Tamson's eyes were too large in her pale face. The girl would suffer grievously if Verity were taken away.

"'Tis the brewer, Thomas," Caleb answered, "and Robert."

"Thee are sure 'tis Thomas?" Hannah couldn't manage more than a whisper.

"Aye. His size and build, and who else would accompany Robert?

Even though she agreed with Caleb, Hannah hated to hear it confirmed.

"Father, you cannot let him—" Boots on the porch stopped Tamson mid-sentence.

Robert entered first, then held the door for Thomas. They were followed by Caleb Jr. and Hannah Jr., who had come in from the barn. Robert's eyes found hers, and there was nothing reassuring in them. No ready smile. The sensitive one of her sons was troubled by whatever was coming. Deeply troubled.

"Caleb, Hannah." Thomas removed his hat.

"Welcome, Thomas," Caleb said.

A welcome was the farthest thing from Hannah's mind, but the manners instilled in her from childhood came forth. "Please, come in and warm thyself by the fire. Hannah Jr., the boys are upstairs if thee would be so kind as to see to them."

"Let Robert have thy coat and enter." Caleb ushered Thomas to the hearth.

Thomas held his hands to the heat. "'Tis a raw morning out there."

"Thee must have been on the road at first light," Caleb said.

"Aye. 'Tis best not to let things fester." Thomas straightened and faced Caleb.

Hannah moved to her husband's side, her fingers finding and twining with his. The warm pressure didn't erase her anxiety, but it helped. Whatever was to come, they would see it through together.

"There are dire things happening in the village." Thomas cleared his throat. "I cannot tell you much, because I know not the extent of it, but there are whispers—nay, more than whispers." He shook his head. "Some of the young girls in the village have started having some type of fits."

Fits?

Hannah's heart lifted. The visit didn't concern Verity at all, but an illness in the village.

"And thee are concerned that it may be contagious?" Caleb asked.

"That and the tendency of some among us to blame you Quakers for things you are not privy to." Thomas looked with regret at Robert. "He is a bright lad and will do well in the craft, but at this time..." He shook his head. "We know not what we are dealing with. Dr. Griggs is past due to arrive. Perhaps he will be able to explain what is happening when he does."

"'Twould be wiser to keep to the farm." Caleb glanced at everyone around the room. "For all of us."

And keeping to the farm would keep Verity out of the Puritans' way as well, which suited Hannah just fine.

Verity took the little boys' favorite toys from the shelf and put them on the floor, a crude wooden horse she'd been told Robert had carved, a leather ball, and a woolen rabbit that looked to be sewn from an old coat. That would entertain them while Verity stood by the door she'd left partly open so she could hear.

Someone coming meant someone might take her away.

It had taken a couple of weeks, but she'd been able to push that worry aside in her happiness with the Buffums. In the past week, it hadn't occurred to her at all, perhaps because they'd not gone to the village for meeting because of the depth of the snow.

Now it all came crashing back.

The dark shack with its dirt floor. The hard wooden shelf with only a thin blanket for warmth. The hunger. The fear.

She wrapped her arms around herself and listened, but the muffled murmur of voices made it impossible to make out their words. As much as she wanted to hear, she would not leave the boys unattended. They couldn't replace the brother and sister she'd lost, but Benji and Jonathan had filled the empty space in her heart. As Hannah and Caleb had filled the empty spaces left by the deaths of Momma, Papa, and Uncle William.

Were they to be taken from her now too? Not in death, but in life?

Footsteps on the stairs shot a tremor through Verity. But it was Hannah Jr. who stepped into the hallway, not a man from the village. Verity ran to her and threw her arms around her. "Will he take me away?"

"I know not." Hannah Jr.'s hug was as fierce as Verity's, and they clung together for a long moment. "Do thee wish to go downstairs? I will stay with the boys."

Did she? If she went down, she'd have to face the truth—whatever it was. Up here in the boys' room, she still felt protected and a part of the family.

Caleb and Hannah had spoken to her several times over the past weeks about the importance of truth. Not just truth about worldly things, which she understood, but about God's truth. His promises to His people. Verity wasn't quite sure she was one of His people, but Caleb had assured her that she could be when she understood enough and was ready. But the importance of truth was the beginning of all that. She needed to want to learn the truth.

Was she brave enough to face it now?

"I think thee should go and listen." Hannah Jr.'s voice wobbled a little. "'Tis better to know than to worry, is it not?"

Was it? Verity glanced toward the stairs, then back at the young woman who had become her big sister in all the ways that mattered. She faced the stairs again and approached them with slow steps, taking care to make as little noise as possible. She glanced back again, drew strength from Hannah Jr.'s nod, then descended the steps, listening as the murmurs became words as she crept closer.

A floorboard squeaked in the quiet that followed Caleb's statement about staying on the farm. Hannah glanced at the doorway to the hall. Verity stood there, back straight, face pale, eyes huge and frightened. Hannah held out her hand, and the girl hurried to her side.

"I hate to lose Robert, even for a little while, with us being so busy," said Thomas. "But 'tis for the best."

"'Tis not forever," Robert said. "I shall return to my apprenticeship when all this has passed."

"As surely it shall." Thomas's voice held a note of hope. "'Twill be found to be nothing in the end, I pray. Just some girlish flights of fancy."

Girlish? The chanting of the girls in the forest—was that a part of which Thomas spoke?

"Please, have a seat." Caleb indicated a chair for Thomas. "Can thee tell us what has happened to bring this fear about?"

"'Tis a puzzlement, for sure, the young girls acting so strangely. I have not seen it myself, but 'tis said they have fallen into fits whereupon they lose all control of themselves and afterward have no memory of it."

Hannah suppressed a shudder lest Verity feel it. The girl had been as disquieted by the chanting in the woods as she had been. Hannah had a good suspicion that it was related to what Thomas had described. Yet to mention the incident, even to a Puritan as friendly as Thomas had been, was too risky. She and Caleb had already lost so much to Puritan suspicion. Hannah would not put her family in jeopardy like that again.

What she really needed to hear was... "So thee have not come for Verity?"

"What?" Thomas looked to her, brows drawn together. Then he appeared to notice the girl beside Hannah. "Nay. Upon my word, nay. 'Twould be best for all involved for her to remain here with you."

Hannah sat in the chair she'd been leaning against, her knees sapped of their strength, but not her arms. She pulled

Verity onto her lap and held her tightly. "Praise God," she breathed against Verity's ear.

"I already did," Verity whispered back.

"And after, when this other matter is put to rest"—Caleb leaned forward—"will Verity be allowed to remain with us?"

Thomas took his time to answer, surveying the kitchen and the people gathered in it. "I cannot think there is a better place for her than this. If 'tis within my powers among the village elders, then I would say aye." He lifted a finger in caution. "But I cannot speak for all."

"Fair enough." Caleb sat back in his chair.

"Pastor Parris would be the major objector, of course, but since 'tis his own daughter and niece who are victims of the bewildering behaviors, I dare say, he has more weighty problems on his mind." Thomas stood and clamped a large hand on Robert's shoulder. "'Tis sorry I am, lad, but I pray this resolves quickly, and we may all resume our peaceful life in the village."

"I look forward to returning." Robert grabbed his coat." I will fetch thy horses around." He slipped out the door.

Her boy was fast becoming a man. Hannah hugged Verity a little tighter.

"And now I must be on my way before I get snowed in out here. Goodie Buffington would not be pleased should I miss her dinner." He gave a short laugh, both hands on his round belly.

"Thank thee for looking after Robert and warning us of what is happening." Caleb rose. "I shall let the other Friends know."

"'Twould perhaps be prudent to avoid the village as much as possible until this thing blows over, as I am sure it shall." Thomas shrugged into his coat. "Dr. Griggs' arrival should see it all put to rights."

Caleb walked out with him as Hannah Jr. entered with Benji and Jonathan.

Tamson raced to Hannah and Verity, arms wrapping around them both. "She is staying! Verity is part of our family now."

The little boys also rushed over. Hannah Jr. following with a dazzling smile. "I am so pleased, Verity."

Hannah's heart was filled with gratitude. Verity might not be with them forever, but she was for now. *Care not then for the morrow, for the morrow shall care for itself: the day hath enough with his own grief.* Hannah would hang onto that wisdom from God.

Verity snuggled under the thick quilt and looked toward the bedside table at the tapered candle holding the darkness at bay. Once she would have been afraid of the darkness when the candle was blown out, but not anymore.

Tamson pulled on her nightcap and slipped into the bed, its strong ropes squeaking under the mattress with her weight. Before she settled down, she blew out the light.

Darkness closed around Verity, but so did Tamson's arm. Verity rolled onto her side, and Tamson curved her body against her, the added warmth chasing the last chill from the clean linens.

"I thanked God tonight for allowing thee to stay." Tamson's breath moved the hairs that had escaped from Verity's nightcap.

"'Tis what I wanted more than anything."

Tamson raised on one elbow, letting in some of the cold air, her face a pale shadow above Verity. "We are truly sisters now, are we not?"

"I... I wish we could be." It was hard to mouth the words that clogged her throat with longing.

"Then I say we can." With a satisfied huff, Tamson burrowed back under the quilt. "I always wanted a younger sister. Not that I love Benji and Jonathan any less, thee understand, but a sister... A sister is something special." She squeezed her arm around Verity. "Thee are something special."

Something special. A sister. A part of a family again. Not her own, not really, but a family that treated her as if she belonged—not as an orphan in need. Certainly not as a rag-picker.

Tamson pressed her cheek to Verity's. "I love thee." Her whisper was heavy with sleepiness.

"I love you—thee—too." With all her heart.

She felt the smile of her new sister against her cheek, and closed her eyes, not the least bit afraid of the dark.

Author's Historical Notes

Yellow fever, which fictional Uncle William succumbed to, made its way into the American Colonies via trade ships carrying slaves from Africa. It became a deadly threat throughout the colonies. Those who contracted the worst form of the disease had a 50/50 chance of survival. The disease-carrying mosquitoes eventually migrated on ships to Europe where great numbers of people died. A cheap and effective vaccine became available in 1940 to eradicate the disease in the U.S. However, it still plagues people in Africa and South America to this day.

The scene in the forest where Betty Parris and Abigail Williams are listening to tales of evil from the West Indies slave woman known as Tituba is taken from a historical account that many believe was the beginning of the occurrences that led to the Salem Witch Trials. Many accounts credit the girls dabbling in the "black magic" of those islands as the source of their original bizarre behavior. Whether people today believe in demonic powers or not, the Puritans certainly did. And there are contemporary stories which eerily parallel the girls' experiences, including one that was memorialized in the movie *The Crucible*.

Another popular theory of the bizarre events that occurred with Betty and Abigail is that the extremely strict upbringing—many say the stifling upbringing—brought about the events. That the suppression an any individuality of thought or expression of the Puritan children caused the girls to act out and behave as they did.

A more modern theory is that a particular type of wheat mold could have been produced that year due to the known weather conditions at that time, and if consumed, that mold has been proven to cause hallucinations. But why it would have been evidenced in only certain family members at a time when most families ate from the same pot or loaf, no one has been able to explain.

Tensions between the Puritans and Quakers are well documented, with Quakers being executed in some instances simply for being Quakers. Puritans came to the American Colonies in the mid-1600s in large numbers to escape widespread religious persecution in Europe. Almost immediately, they began persecuting not only Quakers, but Jews and Catholics as well. It is one of history's greater ironies.

SALEM VILLAGE

BOOK ONE

The
Carpenter

PEGG THOMAS

The Carpenter - Scene 1

January 15, 1692

H AD THEIR IDYLLIC TIME near Salem Village come to an end? The question hounded Caleb Buffum as he hunched over the headboard of a baby's cradle he'd been commissioned to make for a Puritan goodwife in the village. He blew a thin curl of wood from the end of his carving chisel and glanced out the window. Someone approached with her head down, either his wife or his eldest daughter, bundled against the cold until he couldn't be sure which one.

The door to the barn banged shut, and then the inside door leading into the carpentry shop opened.

Hannah Jr. entered the workshop and untied the knitted wool scarf that had covered her head, draping it over her shoulders to expose her dark blond hair covered with her linen cap. "I hope I am not disturbing thee, Father." Snow lingered on the tops of her boots and dusted the hem of her wool skirt. She approached the brazier in the middle of the carpenter shop and held her hands out to its warmth.

"Thee are never a disturbance." Caleb set his chisel aside and dusted off his hands. "What brings thee out in this cold?"

"I am just returned from the village." And by her tone, something hadn't gone well.

Of all his children, Hannah Jr. was the steadiest, the least likely to be worried over the strange goings-on among the Puritans there. "What happened that brings thee out to see me?"

"'Tis more of a feeling than a happening." She picked at a loose thread on her heavy cape. "While many of those in the village are standoffish to me, today was different." Raised blue eyes so like her mother's met his. "They scurried along the street without greetings even for each other and kept their faces down."

"'Tis cold even for January. Perhaps 'twas the wind that hurried them along without greetings." Yet her words struck hard on the tail of his own thoughts.

"I think not just the wind." She spread her hands out, palms up. "On my deliveries, there were no happy greetings. I was handed the coins, the goodwives took their cheese and butter, and then closed the door without a parting word." Then she glanced around at the window and back at him. "Except for the Buffingtons, of course. Sarah is always kind, as are all her children." Her cheeks grew rosy, whether from the brazier's heat or her reaction to those of the village, he couldn't be sure.

Even the goodwives, her loyal clients, had responded as such? That was unusual. At least, it was unusual for Salem Village. In other places, it was common practice. If a Puritan would purchase anything from one of the Friends—those whom they called Quakers—it was grudgingly and with an air of contempt meant to put them in their place.

Caleb remembered that feeling all too well, having faced it too many times. Were they to face them again? Here in the village where they'd made their home for the past twelve years?

"I know Thomas Buffington warned thee of something happening in the village, but I did not expect to feel so..." Hannah Jr. let her words fall off in a shrug.

The Brewer, Thomas, to whom their son, Robert, had been apprenticed, had arrived the week prior with both Robert and the warning. There was something brewing in the village other than his ales, small beers, and ciders. Two of the village girls had fallen into some sort of fits on several occasions, and the cause was as yet unknown. Thomas felt that it would be better for Robert to remain on the farm until whatever it was had passed.

"I was very uncomfortable, Father."

"Thee are wise to be uncomfortable when confronted in such a manner."

Hannah Jr. didn't know of their history. She'd been far too young to remember their escape when he and Hannah had run from a mob of Puritans. Perhaps it was time to tell her. He didn't relish the idea, didn't want to rehash what had happened. But he certainly didn't want Hannah to have to tell their daughter of those dark days. She'd suffered enough because of it. Caleb pulled the two stools he kept in the shop close to the brazier. "Have a seat. I believe 'tis time to tell thee about what happened before."

"Before?" She loosened her cloak and perched on one of the stools, but Caleb paced behind the other one.

"'Twas a long time ago, and thee had just turned a year old a month before. Your mother and I lived outside of a little village not unlike Salem Village in size and population with farms surrounding it, except that the Friends community was smaller there and the Puritans tolerated us even less. In fact, they were openly hostile on many occasions." He stopped and rubbed a hand down his face, seeing the past among the tidy rows of tools lining the back wall of the shop. "A sickness came about in late January of that year, and many people died. Too many. The very young and the very old were hardest hit, of course. We heard of it in our Friends community outside the village, yet none of our people succumbed to the illness."

"How terrible that must have been for those poor people."

He jerked at his daughter's voice. Brought back to the moment, he sat on the stool and took her hand in his. "The Puritans came to believe that the sickness must have been caused by sin, and who better to blame the sin on than we Friends?"

Her cool fingers wrapped around his, her expression filled with empathy.

"The farm closest to the village was that of my best friend. He and his wife had married only months before. He had a nice little flock of sheep and was excited to plant a cabbage crop in the spring. But that never happened." He stopped and searched the trusting depths of his daughter's eyes, wishing he could spare her from the rest. They'd raised their children to be strong and capable, unafraid to try new things and test their ideas as long as they fell within the bounds of the scriptures. He and Hannah hadn't wanted them to grow up under a cloud of fear.

But this one, their eldest, was an adult. Of all of them, she could handle the truth. And it was best coming from him—to spare Hannah the retelling. He also should prepare Hannah Jr. in case they were forced to run again. With such a large family, they would need the oldest children to help with the younger ones.

"What happened, Father?" Concern lined her lovely forehead. If only the world didn't have such darkness in it. If only it could be as it should have been. But *if onlys* were not the world they lived in.

"The Puritans of the village—I know not who or how many—decided that the sin and sickness started among we Friends. Their proof was that none of us had died." He shook his head. "Very few of the Friends had fallen ill at all that winter, and none with the same symptoms as were reported in the village."

"Then how came they to accuse the Friends?" she asked. "That makes no sense."

"As thee know, there has long been hatred from the Puritans toward the Friends." He raised a hand to forestall the comment forming on her lips. "There have also been Friends who have acted to antagonize the Puritans and deepen the resentment they harbor toward us and our differing views of the scriptures." Nothing in life was completely one-sided. Hannah Jr. needed to understand that as well. Even if, at the time of their escape, it had been.

"But to make such a hateful accusation..." She let her thought trail off.

"In their hatred and fear, having convinced themselves that the illness was our fault, they descended on my friend's house and burned it to the ground."

Hannah Jr. pressed her hand over her mouth, her eyes glimmering with a sheen of tears.

Turning his face away from her, he drew in a steadying breath. Even after all the years, the pain remained sharp. Should he tell her the rest? Would it prepare her for what might come? Or would it frighten her unnecessarily?

Give me wisdom, Lord.

He waited until he felt that familiar nudge in his spirit. Then he met her eyes again. "My friend and his wife had been locked inside."

Her gasp knifed through his chest, driving the memory deeper.

"It was just coming on dark when we saw the flames. Several of us from neighboring farms rush to help, only to be shot at and driven away by the Puritans. Two of the Friends fell from the bullets, I learned much later. I was able to make it back to thy mother with nothing more than a bullet hole in the tail of my coat, but we could not stay. Another house was in flames by the time I arrived home." The fear from that moment still burned deep within him. Fear for his wife and child. Fear that he wouldn't be able to save them.

"I turned the cows out and saddled our horse for 'twas safer to ride through the forest than try to escape on the roads. Hannah packed what she could carry, some food and what was needed for thee. Thee were wrapped in a blanket and rode with thy mother while I led the horse away. We could hear the raised cry of the Puritans coming after us." The pictures in his head were so vivid, sweat broke out on his back despite the chill of the shop. "There was no snow on the ground that year, thank the Lord, and they could not track us in the dark."

"Surely the Puritans knew thee would not fight back." Hannah's voice was strained. "How could they attack thee in such a way, with fire and muskets?"

"They were crazed by the loss of their loved ones, I assume. Perhaps chased by the very devil they so fear."

Hannah clung to his hand. "But thee made it safely away."

They almost had. He couldn't tell her the rest. He'd told her all she needed to know. Enough to understand what had befallen them and what could befall them again if things in the village turned bad.

"We had lost everything but what we carried and the horse. His name was Samson and he was black. Funny how I remember that, but it probably helped us escape into the darkness. He was a good horse. I was forced to sell him when we arrived at Salem Town for enough money to pay rent and purchase food. I found employment with a carpenter there. We saved until we could purchase this farm."

"I remember the tiny log cabin in Salem Village. The door rattled in the wind."

"Aye, and it seemed I had to patch the roof every other week to keep ahead of the leaks." He'd worked night and day and saved every penny to move them out of that cabin. Hannah had skimped on even necessities to help. Caleb Jr. and Robert had been born there, but they'd been able to move to the farm before Tamson arrived, by less than a month if he remembered correctly. During the last twelve years, they'd built a successful farm and carpentry and been blessed with two more boys. And lately, another girl, although she'd arrived as an eight-year-old and not a babe, an orphan in need of a family.

A Puritan orphan.

Would the decision to take her into their home turn into something their family would suffer for? Would the village Puritans see that—along with whatever illness was upon them—as a reason to drive them out? Or burn them down?

The Carpenter will release
September 2, 2025
It's available
for **preorder on Amazon**

Reviews are Golden

Reviews are the lifeblood of authors. Leaving a review on **Amazon**, **Goodreads**, and/or **BookBub** means that more readers will find our books! Reviews can be long or short - your honest opinion of the book. Shout-outs on any social media platforms also help!

About Pegg Thomas

A lifelong history geek, Pegg Thomas lives in Michigan's Upper Peninsula with Michael, her husband of *mumble* years. She creates American stories with real history and fictional characters inspired by her ancestors who immigrated here in the early 1600s. When not working or writing, Pegg can be found in her garden, her kitchen, or sitting at one of her antique spinning wheels creating yarn to turn into her signature wool shawls.

Pegg won the 2019 FHL Readers' Choice Award for novellas, was a double-finalist for the 2019 ACFW Carol Award for novellas, and a finalist for the 2019 ACFW Editor of the Year. She was a finalist in the 2021 FHL Readers' Choice Award for novellas. Pegg won the 2022 Selah Award for historical romance and placed 2nd with her second entry. She was also a finalist for the 2023 Selah Award, placed 2nd for the 2024 Selah Award, and won two 2024 Will Roger's Medallion Awards. Pegg spent 3 ½ years as the managing editor of Smitten Historical Romance.

PeggThomas.com
Facebook
Goodreads
BookBub
Amazon
https://www.subscribepage.com/PeggThomas (newsletter signup)